DEAL WITH THE DEVIL
BOOK FIVE

Ride
with the
Devil

CARIN HART

For those of you who see the world we're living in and would rather watch it burn...

...along with a sexy and sweet driver who's there to pour the gasoline and grin as his girl strikes the match.

FOREWORD

Thank you for checking out *Ride with the Devil*!

At the end of *Dance with the Devil*, Cross da Silva's tattoo parlor was burned down with him inside of it. Though he survived—and got his revenge on the man who was responsible for the fire—he couldn't understand why a crystal hummingbird in a fireproof box was left inside the ruins. That leads us to this book! It begins the night of that fateful fire, and will reference events from the previous book (including the the crystal hummingbird, plus Luca's undercover stint, pretending to work for Johnny Winter while plotting to break Cross and Genevieve out of captivity).

This is also the end of the main **Deal with the Devil** series. There will be other throwbacks to people and events that happened since the beginning, but my main focus with this book was telling the story of Luca and Kylie's romance—and having a ton of fun with a killer FMC, the quiet driver MMC who's been behind the wheel the whole series (and deserves a chance to shine), and ending the series with a bang (both literally and figuratively!).

So, buckle up! Luca is unlike any hero I've written before (and not just because he's a repressed virgin who is instantly obsessed with Kylie). Same with the Hummingbird... I went into this book knowing that I wanted an unrepentant, murderous heroine who makes no apologies for who she is, and I only hope you love her as much as I do!

Ride with the Devil includes: instalove; insta-obsession; unprotected sex acts; masturbation; anal; religious trauma that still affects the MMC; drugging; kidnapping; captivity; poison; inappropriate use of a vegetable; a virgin MMC with repressed urges; an unhinged heroine assassin with no boundaries; murder, on and off page; discussions of child abuse (including visible scars left behind on the MMC), as well as mentions of domestic violence (happening to the FMC's sister), drugs, sex work, and plenty of guns.

If you choose to read, please enjoy!

xoxo,
Carin

TEN COMMANDMENTS

1. ~~I am the Lord thy God. Thou shall not have any strange gods before Me.~~
2. ~~Thou shall not take the name of the Lord thy God in vain.~~
3. ~~Remember to keep holy the Lord's day.~~
4. ~~Honor thy father and mother.~~
5. Thou shall not kill.
6. Thou shall not commit adultery.
7. ~~Thou shall not steal.~~
8. ~~Thou shall not bear false witness against thy neighbor.~~
9. ~~Thou shall not covet thy neighbor's wife.~~
10. ~~Thou shall not covet thy neighbor's goods.~~

PROLOGUE

KYLIE

Some people kill because they have the urge. They're twisted, or they're evil.

Me? I kill because it's *fun*.

Money's good, too. Money's fucking *great*. Do you know how much people will pay to get rid of somebody they hate? And not even *hate* sometimes. You'd be amazed how often my clients will give me a target for the most ridiculous and asinine reasons.

Do I care what they are? Nope. As long as I have the cash in hand or the full amount wired into one of my three offshore accounts when I'm done, I don't give a shit about their petty justifications. Though, I'll admit, I get a better sense of satisfaction if the hit is on an asshole.

I live to eliminate assholes.

Too bad I'm a little iffy on tonight's target.

Whenever I take a job, I get my kicks putting a little spin on it. I get the name, research the name, and pick a way to kill them that screams poetic justice. At the beginning of my career, I went with a gun nine times out of ten. That was too easy before long. Where's the pizazz, right? Where's the statement?

Where's the signature?

Some little girls grow up and want to be a teacher or a ballerina or a homemaker. Not baby Kylie. I didn't know what the hell I wanted to do until I shot my dad's .22 and made my first kill. And while that was a clear-cut case of self-defense—and, as a wide-eyed, baby-faced sixteen-year-old, no one would've believed I *wanted* Jason to die—something sparked to life inside of me that day. Now, a decade later, I've made this my career, and I'm pretty damn good at it.

I'm the Hummingbird. And while I know that my chosen name wasn't picked out to strike fear into those I'm gunning for, the fact that anyone who knows it *will* be frightened... hey. I get my kicks where I can, and I love how such a seemingly innocent bird can mean death.

Hummingbirds are fast. They're light. They have big brains, an impressive memory, and are surprisingly territorial.

Plus, I found a box of, like, three hundred hummingbird crystal figurines at a yard sale back in Westfield when I was seventeen, and was just dying for some way to use them. At the time, I never thought they'd be my signature—the token I leave behind at every kill to take credit for the hit—but hey... waste not, want not, right?

I have one in my 'go' bag right now. Looking like an oversized canvas tote, my bag is slung over my shoulder. My wild, curly hair is currently tamed by the pair of over-the-ear headphones I have on. I'm not playing any music through the speakers since I need to hear my surroundings, but they're a perfect addition to my costume.

Between my artfully ripped jeans, the light hooded sweatshirt that would be overkill during a mid-July afternoon but perfect for the late hour, my bag, and my headphones, I look like a mid-twenties art student rushing home after a late night out. Taking the trip down Third Avenue, passing the shops—all closed now—that a woman like me would patronize, before reaching the apartments in this part of the West Side of Springfield.

Only I don't live in Springfield. Don't live anywhere, really, since putting down roots would make it easier to get nabbed by those looking to cage up the Hummingbird. I usually find a hotel or two—trading halfway throughout my stay—when I'm plotting a hit, then blowing town as soon as the job is done.

I've staked this street out enough over the last two weeks to know that it's empty once the stores all close up. The costume is just in case, and because while I might have a need for adrenaline and a bit of a death wish, my rep is everything to me. I've been in the hitwoman business for four years now, and all it will take is one sloppy kill for the jobs to stop coming. So I have a healthy bank account already. You can't take it with you, but I can make sure I have enough to enjoy myself before I go.

I'm meeting my client here in about fifteen minutes. Knowing how much of a hard-on he has for this, I wouldn't be surprised if he shows up earlier. I'll tack on an added fee if he does—I don't work with an audience—but for the moment, at least, everything is quiet.

Calm.

Not for much longer.

Hefting up my tote, sensing the slosh of the liquid in its canister, I slow my roll until I'm standing just outside of my target: Sinners and Saints tattoo shop.

The guy who hired me for this hit, Mickey Kelly, claimed that Carlos 'Cross' da Silva was a creep who forced himself on an innocent virgin, and when Mickey tried to stop him from raping the girl, the cruel tattooist lunged at him, his teeth taking a chunk out of the poor guy's dick.

Now, I'm not an idiot. There are so many holes in his story, it's like a slice of Swiss cheese. To get the tip of his cock bitten off, that implies he was waving his dick around—so maybe it wasn't da Silva who was planning on assaulting this Libellula chick. Then again, Kelly said it was, and he was willing to pay me a cool fifteen grand upfront to get rid of a predator.

For fifteen grand now, fifteen grand transferred after I leave behind my hummingbird and Kelly verifies that da Silva's dead, if the guy says da Silva needs to die, I've got it.

And, like always, I'm going to have fun with it.

The hummingbird figurines aren't my only signature, even if they're the most obvious ones. When the time allows for it—and the client is okay with it—I like to tailor my kills to the targets. Especially if they seem like they're a trash person, it amuses me to know that the way I off them is personal.

Just like tonight's will be.

I did my research. Back when da Silva was a kid, his family died in a fire. He survived, so did his stepfather, but his mother and two siblings died. The stepfather eventually got fingered for setting the blaze, but there were enough questions at the time that made it seem Carlos was in on it, too.

Even if he wasn't, he's a Sinner. Literally.

A member of the Sinners Syndicate, a mafia local to this big city, da Silva is their official tattoo artist. I haven't fucked with the gangs in Springfield before, but once I leave my hummingbird behind, these hotshots will at least know I'm flitting around.

I look forward to it.

The front door is shut, a neon *closed* sign crackling in the window. Over my head, the lights are out. I hung out in my rental car earlier tonight, waiting for the blondie he's shacking up with to leave before da Silva locked the door behind her. Now I'm banking on him being asleep in his bed alone.

Genevieve Libellula. The woman that Kelly claimed da Silva assaulted has been spending nearly every night in the apartment that da Silva keeps over his shop, and another reason why my gut feeling is iffy on this one. If he really held her down and fucked her in front of Kelly, would she keep crawling back to him? Unless this is some kind of Stockholm syndrome thing...

I know all about that. Lindy kept returning to Jason no matter how many times he hurt her because she loved him, even as she cradled her busted arm and put a pound of make-up on to hide the bruises. She would've loved him to her own death if I hadn't shot him first, and if another woman needs help getting away from her abuser, I'm more than willing to help.

Just in case, I take the corner, dipping around to the back of the studio. Rear doors fill the back, as do trash cans and wider delivery areas for the shops. There's also a handful of fire escapes attached to places with more than one floor. I already know which one belongs to da Silva. I jog toward it, then take the stairs two at a time to reach the top.

The window is closed, the shade only halfway drawn. It's dark in there, and while I can't see if da Silva has any guests over, odds are that the artist is sleeping, blissfully unaware of what's about to happen to him.

I smile and grab a tube of industrial glue from my supplies.

I don't waste time fiddling with it. After unscrewing the cap, I slather as much of the glue in the tube as I can into the gap where the window pane touches the sill. I push down at the top, counting to twenty until I'm sure it's good and stuck, and re-cap the glue.

Can't give him any easy way out if he wakes up before the fire does its job.

Bouncing back down the stairs, the metal creaking under my weight, I touch down on the pavement before the sound carries too far.

I scoot around to the front. Still no one on the street, and I stroll back to Sinners and Saints. Grabbing my lock-pick set from my bag, I get to work breaking into the studio. I've practiced on the same style lock in my hotel room. My record was forty-two seconds. With the real thing, I'm popping it open in less than thirty.

I'm prepared for an alarm to sound, though I don't expect it to. Why rely on the cops when a Sinner can handle a break-in on their own? That's what cockiness gets you, and as I slip inside the eerily quiet studio, I grin when I realize I am right.

I give myself one minute to get in and out. By the time the door is closing behind me, I already have the gloves on and the canister of gasoline open. Humming a song under my breath, I move around the studio, sprinkling the accelerant all over so that the fire catches and catches quickly. Pushing past the door that divides the studio from the stairs, I sprinkle some near the bottom one, but don't bother going up where da Silva lives. For one, I want him to realize he's trapped in there before the flames get him. For another, I've already wasted thirty of my seconds.

Tossing the canister in the studio, I yank off my gloves so that I don't have any of the gasoline on me. They get discarded, too, more kindling for the fire. With my hands free, I grab the fireproof box I bought for just the occasion, plus the matchbook I palmed from Il Sogno, a restaurant frequented by the Dragon-flies on the East End of the city. If it survives the flames, it wouldn't hurt to cast a little suspicion on Damien Libellula, the leader of the Sinners' rival gang —and Genevieve's older brother.

Still humming, bopping my head to a song only I can hear—no headphones required—I strike a match and drop it into the first pool of gasoline I find. With ten seconds to go, I drop the fireproof box containing my hummingbird just inside the doorway and slip back out into the night.

I'm not going to stick around. Usually, I do. I won't get paid if I don't complete the job, but how exactly can da Silva survive *that*? And that's assuming he even wakes up before the smoke gets him.

But I'm pretty sure I saw Kelly lurking across the street as I slipped back out. Hey. If the client wants a front-row seat to my work now that I'm done, I'm not going to stop him. He saw enough to know that I was here. I'll get paid.

And if I don't? I'll cut the rest of his cock off and feed it to him for even trying to think of stiffing me— and if he knows enough of my reputation to track me down and hire me, he'll know *that*, too.

So I leave. As the dark interior becomes orange from the glow of the blooming flames, I adjust the headphones, brush a stray curl out of my face, and head back the way I came.

As I go, I smile a little wider, singing along to the song that's been bouncing around in my head since I struck the match.

"'Come on baby, light my fire'..."

thou shall not...

卌 III

ONE
WHEELS

LUCA

FIVE MONTHS LATER

There's nowhere I'd rather be than behind the wheel.

I got a late start at driving. My parents convinced me that I wasn't legally allowed to get a license until I was twenty-one; if I hadn't pushed the subject, it might have been even later. Having been homeschooled my entire life, I didn't realize that most of my peers got their permits at seventeen, their licenses at eighteen. I just saw it as my chance to escape, and I was desperate enough to take whatever opportunity I could.

Of course, just because they finally allowed me to learn, that didn't mean I had a car of my own. I stole theirs after they disowned me, using the twenty-year-old Buick to get me from my hometown all the way to Hamilton, a day-and-a-half's drive away, then traded it away for a cheap, broken-down Mustang that I built back up, piece by piece.

That car is my pride and joy even now, five years after I got it to run. I have it stowed in the garage of the apartment building where I live, taking it out for special occasions. I have a discreet black Sedan Devil gave me on my first anniversary of getting my Sinners tattoo that I use when the boss doesn't need me. Other than that, I'm driving his town car for him.

That's because I have one job as a Sinner: the Devil of Springfield's personal driver. I take him wherever he has to go, whenever he needs to be there. I'm always on the clock, and I like it that way. I like being useful, and it's not as if I have a personal life of my own.

Not anymore.

Tonight is one of the scheduled dinners that Devil has with the head of the Libellula Family. They trade off locations. One meal, it's on Sinner turf; the next, it's on Dragonfly territory. It's Damien's turn to host.

Devil always offers to let me sit down to a meal while I wait for him to finish his. No matter where the dinner's being held, you can bet that half the clientele is made up of Sinners and Dragonflies, each one there to watch the back of their leader. Just because we have a truce these days, that doesn't mean it could change at any moment.

It's possible. When I arrived in Springfield, the two rival gangs were already years into a feud that started when a Dragonfly girl got shot and died in Rolls McIntyre's arms. I was also waiting in the car when Damien Libellula took Devil's wife, Ava, and blackmailed the boss into agreeing to a truce. It's been shaky at best since then, but now that the Sinners and the Dragonflies have a shared enemy in Johnny Winter and his Snowflakes... who knows? Maybe the truce *will* last.

It's still awkward as fuck, eating a plate of pasta or a bloody steak, on edge to see if guns are going to be drawn before dessert. I'd much rather hang out in the car, then grab myself something from a drive-thru after Devil relieves me for the night.

It didn't take long for him to figure that out. So while he stopped with the invitations, he also gave me permission to drive around instead of parking out front to wait for him. So long as I'm there when he needs me —and he'll text me with enough time to get back to the restaurant—I'm free to do what I want while he's stuck with Libellula.

On the West Side, there's a lot more I can accomplish. Tonight, we're on the East End. Dragonfly territory. We might have a truce, but all it will take is the wrong Dragonfly seeing my devil tat to start shit. I'd rather stick to Sinner turf if I can.

But since I can't...

There's one spot on the edge of the East End where all Sinners are welcome: Sinners and Saints II, the rebuilt tattoo studio owned and operated by Cross da Silva, the Sinners' official tattooist.

He used to own a spot on Third Avenue. Last summer, some asshole who worked for Johnny Winter decided to get back at Cross by burning down his place while he was sound asleep in the apartment above it.

Fucked up, right? Poor guy was taken captive by Winter's goons, along with Damien's sister, Genevieve. Trapped behind bars for three weeks until the two gangs—with the help of yours truly—worked together to break them out of Winter's containment facility in Hamilton, he was just starting his fledgling relationship with Genevieve when a blast from their past settled on a little arson for fun.

Thou shall not kill...

Luckily, Cross made it out in one piece. The asshole didn't. Neither did Cross's studio. It was nothing but shattered glass, ashes, and melted remains by the time the SFD put the blaze out. Three months after that, though, Cross had a bigger studio built—and because he's in a committed relationship with Genevieve, a professional ballerina who has her own practice room in the same space, it's technically on Dragonfly land.

Her overprotective older brother insisted. A Libellula stays on the East End, even if the ring on her finger says she'll be a da Silva before long. Devil let the relocation slide, and now there's somewhere I can go when I'm stuck on this side of Springfield.

The only vehicle in the side parking area is a motorcycle. Cross's bike. That means he's in even if the *closed* neon in the front of his shop is on.

Sinners have an open invitation to any property run by one of us. I rarely take any of the others up on that, but Cross... he's different.

We've been pals since the first time I asked him to tattoo me. Not the devil tat. We all get those. But I had one in particular in mind, and when I went to Cross to do it, there was no denying that I'd been through some shit.

Cross is his nickname. He says it has nothing to do with religion; though Devil is a lapsed Catholic, and I'm agnostic now, Cross is pretty much an atheist. That's because he has trauma of his own, too, and as much as two straight guys with issues can, we bonded over that.

Because Cross is his nickname—but I have a cross of my own that I can never, ever get rid of.

I can make it my own, though, and with eight simple slashes, I have... and that's all thanks to the syndicate artist.

Through the front window, I can see Cross sitting by himself. His floppy hair is brushed out of his face as he sits behind the desk, legs propped up, boots resting on top of the cleared desktop while he fiddles with something held gingerly between his grip.

I knock on the front door, catching his attention.

His head shoots up, dark eyebrows drawn together as he peers through the glass. He has the light on inside, and despite how dark it is behind me, he must recognize that it's a friend because he raises his voice and calls out, "It's open. Come on in."

I pull open the door, appreciating the blast of heat as it warms my face. The soft lull of faraway music hits my ears at the same time as the astringent scent of the sterilized studio right behind Cross.

Beyond that, there's a door. And though I can't see beyond *that*, the music tells me that Cross's fiancée is somewhere back there, dancing.

I was here two months ago, shortly after they moved into the place. Genevieve was dancing then, too, and I remarked on the soft music tinkling its way out to the front of the tattoo studio. Even with the door separating the two rooms, you can hear it, and Cross told me that was on purpose. They could've sound-proofed her dance studio, but he likes hearing the music she was performing to, so they didn't.

It's great seeing those two so happy. Especially since I can't shake the memory of being led down to the cells and finding the two of them together after all those weeks of captivity. And if that was bad, knowing that Genevieve was forced to pull the trigger and shoot Noah while I was on the upper floor, clearing it so that

Savannah—Damien's assassin wife—and I could break Cross and Genevieve out is even worse.

Thou shall not kill...

...unless you have to.

Cross nods at me. "Let me guess. Boss is on this side of town for dinner?"

"Yup."

"Thought so. Genevieve was supposed to have dinner at the house with her brother and cousin tonight. He cancelled last minute, said Family biz came up. Damien's gotten better. He only shuts my butterfly out when it has something to do with Winter. If Devil's with him, maybe they finally got a lead."

That would be great. Not like I'm afraid of him gunning for me, but I did go undercover, using my time as a criminal in Hamilton to get an interview with Winter's crew. I got the job on Devil's orders once our tech genius, Tanner, figured out that was where Cross was being held, and I betrayed my 'new' boss when the four us escaped, leaving a body in our wake.

Does that mean Winter will come after me? Maybe. He knows my name, knows some of my history. Still, he's got bigger fish to fry, and since no one's seen hide nor hair of the bastard since Devil and Libellula beat him at his own game, I'm not afraid.

I'm only afraid of one thing, and it's such a leftover from my childhood, I wish I could get over it—but I can't, and that's my shit to deal with.

Fuck knows that we all have our own baggage.

Cross, definitely, but with Genevieve at his side, he's dealing.

Maybe, one of these days, I'll be able to forget Emily completely and finally find a woman who makes me as happy as Genevieve does Cross...

Shrugging my shoulders, moving so that I'm standing in front of the reception desk, I watch Cross's long, slender fingers twirl the item between them.

"What's that you got there?" I jerk my chin at the tiny figurine he's holding onto. It's about an inch, inch-and-a-half high, shimmering pinks and purples sparkling beneath the fluorescent lights as he spins it.

"I've been trying to figure this stupid thing out for months." Cross flicks the crystal with his fingertip before tossing it onto the desk. It hits it with a soft *clink*, and I can tell that it's a figurine of a tiny bird. "Tanner thinks he might be closer to figuring it out. You hear about the Hummingbird, wheels?"

Wheels. Cross is big on nicknames, especially those he gives out himself. Like how he refers to Rolls— already an established nickname for our fixer, Royce McIntyre—as 'sunshine' because of his blond hair and charming personality, or how Genevieve is his 'butter-fly'. Up until last summer, I was just the driver, Cross the artist, but then I risked my neck to help him escape Winter and now I'm 'wheels'.

I shake my head.

He looks surprised. "Really? Not even from Devil in the backseat?"

"I learned a long time ago to block out anything that happens back there," I admit.

Cross chuckles. "Yeah. I've heard about the drives the boss likes to take with his wife. Smart man." Shifting in his seat, he swings his boots down, letting them hit the floor. "So what's up? You need another tat?" Cross gives a little smirk, brushing a lock of hair out of his eye. "Coveting my wife, Luca? Got eyes for Genevieve? Is that number nine?"

I think of the tally marks on my forearm. There are only eight, not ten, and considering what the last two I'm missing stand for, I doubt I'll be completing the set any time soon; not while I'm a driver instead of one of the Sinners responsible for wet work, like Killian or Max.

And I know Cross is teasing. As possessive as he is of the tiny blonde ballerina, he wouldn't be smirking like that if he honestly believed I was interested in his fiancée. He'd be dead serious, and I would probably just be dead.

That's Sinners for you. Fanatically loyal to our leader, but commit to a woman, and she becomes your entire world.

It happened to the boss when he reunited with his childhood sweetheart. Rolls and his wife, Nicolette. Killian and Jasmine. Now Cross and Genevieve.

Maybe it's a good thing that I've never found someone to replace Emily...

Eight tallies. There are only two people in this

world who know why I have them: me and Cross. Mainly because he was the artist who gave me the first five, but by the time I went back for the sixth, then the seventh, and finally the eighth... even the notoriously quiet Cross had to ask if the marks had any particular meaning.

Makes sense. In our line of work, it happens. Like how the Dragonfly enforcers tattoo the back of their biceps with a small leaf every time they kill for their leader. I'm the driver. What could my marks stand for?

Simple: which of the Ten Commandments I've broken.

I grew up a member of the Holy Church of Jesus Devotion. It wasn't until I was free from their hold on me that I realized that the JD part of HCoJD didn't stand for 'Jesus Devotion' like my parents insisted. It stands for Jack Donovan, the pastor and 'prophet' who reigns over the congregation.

Because it's not a church. It's a fucking cult, and I'm still twisted up from all of its teachings.

My tattoo is proof of that. So is the one thing I wish I could stop being afraid of...

Ten Commandments. Ten rules I was beaten into submission into following. Because if I broke all ten, I was sentencing myself to eternal damnation... and even as a twenty-seven-year-old Sinner, I can't bring myself to break *all* the rules, just in case brimstone and hellfire will be waiting for me when I eventually die.

But as long as I only break *nine*...

I got five when I decided to have a physical representation of my count. Some of those were long-broken, as my exacting parents would have told me if I was still in contact with them.

The first time I willingly refused to attend any kind of service on a Sunday? That was number six.

When I realized that I put Devil before any God? Number seven.

And coveting my neighbor's goods... I couldn't help myself last year when my upstairs neighbor parked his brand new, impeccably restored Corvette Stingray alongside my latest half-built passion project.

But coveting my neighbor's wife? I broke that one when I was still under Donovan's control—and knowing that he purposely chose my girl to be his bride was the last straw that kept me there.

"Nah. I'm still at eight," I tell him. "Just thought I'd hang out here while waiting for the boss. You mind?"

He shakes his head. "Genevieve is rehearsing for *Romeo and Juliet*. They open in three weeks, right after the new year. Until then, it's just me and my iPad out here, waiting for her to throw me a bone every now and then."

"That's right. She got the lead role, didn't she?"

A look of pride flashes across his features. "She did. And I expect you to catch a performance before it closes, wheels."

I'm not much of a ballet guy, but I'll be there for these two. "Yeah. Of course."

Cross's dark eyes twinkle. "Maybe we can get Devil to go, too. Have Mona watch baby Claire so he can take Ava out for the night."

I chuckle. "Have Genevieve pass the invite on to Mrs. Crewes. If Ava asks, you'll get Devil's butt in a seat. Promise."

There isn't anything the Devil of Springfield won't do for his beloved wife.

"Good idea. I'll make sure to do that. Maybe we can buy out the whole theatre for the night and have a Sinners-only showing for my butterfly." Cross pauses for a moment. "And a couple of Dragonflies, too, I guess, since Gen wants her brother and Vin to come."

And, like the boss, there isn't anything *Cross* won't do for his butterfly.

I start to open my mouth, maybe make a comment about how far the rivalry between the Sinners and the Dragonflies' has come in the past year-and-a-half when my phone starts buzzing. One, two, three, four texts in rapid succession.

I know it has to be the boss. Not only does Devil send texts the way he speaks—short sentences, straight to the point, so terse you can almost hear the growl in his voice—but I don't really get that many messages on my phone. I lost contact with any of the old crew in Hamilton, and while I've worked as a loyal Sinner in Springfield for three years now, if I'm not with Devil, I'm working on my latest project by myself.

Rolls keeps offering to put me in touch with his

cousin, Jake. A trained mechanic, he actually went to school for the trade instead of picking it up as he went along like I did. Jake lives in Merrill Grove with his new wife, and he'd be willing to help me get parts and shit, but... I don't know. I like Rolls. He's a great guy. His cousin probably is, too.

But I'm used to being alone. Can't say that I *like* it, but I'm used to it.

Just like I'm used to Devil's commands.

I read the messages, stomach twisting when I get to the third one, my head nodding as I hit the fourth.

BOSS

> I'm leaving here in five, but I'm not heading home

> Need to have a meet with Collins. Blockbuster.

> Fucker is bought by the Snowflakes

> Line the trunk

Line the trunk... I know exactly what that means. And if Devil wants me to take care of that before I pick him up at dinner, he's not waiting around for Rolls to take care of clean-up duty like usual. Between the boss and me, we're going to do it ourselves.

Then again, if the vice mayor betrayed the Sinners... he deserves everything he has coming to him.

Will do

Cross raises his eyebrows as soon as I send my reply. "Gotta go?"

"Yup." I pocket my phone, swapping it for my keys so I can head on out. But first... "You don't happen to have any extra tarps lying around, do you?"

TWO
THE DEVIL'S PLAYGROUND

KYLIE

I told myself I would have to be super bored, plus offered the shot at a high-profile hit, to drag my ass back to Springfield. Especially after what happened last time.

See, I don't like to fail. I pride myself on completing every job, no matter what. Finding out that, against all odds, Carlos da Silva survived the fire? That pissed me off. I would've done a u-ey, marched right over to the West Side again, and finished the job if it wasn't for the fact that my client seemed to fall off the face of the planet the same night.

Mickey Kelly never paid me the second half of my commission. Way I saw it back in July, I did what the first fifteen grand bought him. For the second fifteen grand, I'd go after da Silva again—but Kelly disappeared. Considering I left him lurking around Sinners and Saints as the fire caught, I wouldn't be surprised if da Silva got to him first.

After all, the artist made it out in one piece. Kelly vanished. It doesn't take an experienced hitwoman to put two and two together and figure out that the Sinner 86ed my client. At least I got my first fifteen thousand, and when I dug a little deeper and discovered that my suspicions were right, that Kelly was the one who went after the Libellula chick while da Silva only did what he did to protect her, I wrote off the failed hit and the big criminal hotspot of Springfield.

It's been five months. I've pulled off four successful hits since, but the last one was right around Halloween. I made it all the way to Thanksgiving without a job—and then, two weeks ago, Johnny Winter came calling.

Winter runs a nationwide enterprise of crooks, thugs, chemists, and gun runners. Though his home base is in Nevada, the aptly named Snowflakes are spread out from coast to coast. There's a cadre in nearly every state, with their fingers in every single enterprise you can think of.

Guns? They sell them.

Girls? They traffic them.

Drugs? Winter has his own lab set up to develop the most dastardly, addictive junk on the market. He also takes shit that already has a rep—like the new designer drugs of choice, Breeze and Eclipse—and laces them with his concoctions to make it deadly as hell.

I should know. I bought a bad batch from one seller to target another in Camden after his dirty shit killed a couple of middle schoolers. Not as fast-acting as the strychnine I keep on me as a backup plan, but it was a gnarly way to go.

And he fucking deserved it. I don't often take charity cases, and while I'll go to my grave believing that I'm a hedonistic bitch who just wants to find pleasure before I go, I have a couple of hot buttons.

Stuck in a DV relationship? The Hummingbird will get you out of it.

Kids are involved? I don't give a shit if they're assholes, I'm on their side.

Winter's chems might've made the product that caused those tweens to OD. Fuck knows, my latest client has done enough to earn a target on his back. My own sense of morals says that he didn't take those kids' crumpled twenties and sold them the Eclipse that killed them. So I offed the dealer at a discount, then later accepted Winter's contract on a dentist that fucked him over without batting an eye—even if I did nod when I saw how much he was willing to pay.

This past year, Winter had set his sights on Springfield. Word on the street is that he wants a slice of the Libellula Family's counterfeiting ring. That's just an excuse. Johnny Winter wants revenge, and he's convinced that, to get it, he needs to eliminate both the

Sinners Syndicate and the Libellula Family before turning their former territory into his East Coast headquarters.

I knew all that. Kelly heard of my rep through Winter, just like I knew Winter's rep through some of the clients I've worked for these past couple of years before he hired me himself. Winter's the one I got in contact with when Kelly up and disappeared on me—and the one who had no problem telling me the truth about what one of his former goons was up to while Carlos da Silva and Genevieve Libellula were Winter's... guests.

Guests. Right.

And I'm the Queen of Sheba.

Not like I give a shit what Winter does to get ahead. That's why I jumped at the chance to do a job for him when I was just starting out—well, his twin, and that's some other weird thing I don't really get because he was Jimmy, now he's Johnny, and it seems like there were *two* of them before Damien Libellula offed Winter's twin—plus the new leader of the Snowflakes hired me for two of my four most recent kills. All I care about now is that Winter's money comes through on time, and he's generous, too. Like me, the second Winter gets his kicks at my poetic justice, and he'll throw me some extra bucks if I amuse him.

Johnny Winter is as sick and twisted as I am, and I almost decided it would be fun to seduce him and see what he was like in the sack. The fact that, during our sporadic meetings, I got the feeling that he'd rather gut me and see what my insides looked like over experiencing how tight I was wrapped around his cock kept me from pursuing my curiosity about the gang leader. I'll take his money and find my pleasure with the nobodies I pick up between jobs for one-night stands.

I usually troll the local hotspots. Bars, sometimes, or maybe nightclubs. I know what I look like. Depending on how I wear my hair or what outfit I pull on, I could be that sweet-faced innocent in over her head or an experienced woman just out for a good time, looking to end the night even better. It's easy to get attention when I want it, but in my line of work, it pays to be able to blend into the surroundings when I need to.

Like now.

It's mid-December. I pulled on my leather jacket over a deep red sweater, plus a pair of tight dark blue jeans that are molded around the curve of my ass. Black boots so that I don't slip on the icy remnants of an early snowstorm from two days ago. My curls are loose, though I pinned the front pieces back to show off my expertly made-up face.

The turquoise neons around the nightclub are amplified by the white Christmas lights strung up all over the place. The air pulses with the rich beat of the electronic song blasting out of the speakers; no 'Silent Night' or 'Jingle Bells' here, despite the nod to the season in the Christmas lights and the red bows plastered to the edge of the bar top. While some of the city folk are out there, visiting Santa Claus and getting their holiday shopping done, you wouldn't know it was well into December by the warmth in the club or the half-dressed dancers writhing on the floor.

Carrying a barely touched cocktail in my hand, I weave around them, edging toward the tables surrounding the dance floor. I've already had to tell three guys to buzz off since I've been here, and my poor libido is telling me that I should've at least taken one of them up on their offer to either go upstairs or find a little privacy in the club's bathroom.

But I'm not here to get laid. I'm on the job, and since I'm in Springfield again to do another hit for Johnny Winter, it's a biggie.

I'm happy to do it, too. Not only did Winter bump up my fee for me, but I'll take any excuse not to have to return home for Christmas. My parents and my sister have no idea what I do—just that my work has me constantly traveling—but Lindy always gets mopey around the holidays.

Ten years later, and happily married to Charlie for three of them, and she still grieves for the bastard who nearly beat her to death before I took care of him for her. It's almost enough to make me want to dig Jason up and shoot him again to see if that'll finally shake his hold on my older sister.

Maybe I don't get it. Maybe it's because I've never been in love like that before. So desperate to be with one person that you'll overlook everything... and who the fuck am I kidding? That bastard groomed her, beat her, and convinced Lindy that she loved him. If *that*'s love? Then I'm glad I've never found someone to take my heart.

My pussy? Sure. My body? I'll give that to anyone who wants it. It's just sex. I like to experience pleasure, and I'll reward any guy who gets me off first. But *love*?

I'm good.

That's why I'll wait and visit the family in Florida in the new year. Lindy will be back to her bubbly self, my parents will be relieved I stopped by at all, and I'll lie about what I've been up to all while waiting for my next client to reach out...

Right now, I'm booked. Winter gave me a name and a deadline, and I've spent the last week and a half in Springfield—goddamn Springfield—working toward that December 25th deadline.

I told you. Johnny Winter is as broken as I am. Not only does he want one of the most well-known figures in Springfield dead in a way that won't get back to him —not while he's biding his time, making it seem as if the Snowflakes have moved on to New York City instead—but he wants the man eliminated before Christmas.

It's easier said than done. Because while everyone in the city knows my target, it's not easy to get to a man like that... which is why I'm currently spending my

Thursday night at the Devil's Playground. If luck's on my side, I might run into him.

Last night, I partied on the East End, hoping that one or more of the Dragonflies I cozied up to would drop his name. Pretending to be tipsy—but not drunk enough that I went home with any of last night's marks —I danced around the subject, but either they were well-trained or too low in the Family hierarchy to help me.

Same thing with my trip to Springfield City Hall, the courthouse, and even the local library. No dice.

This is my second trip to the Devil's Playground. Rumors run that my target has been spotted here. And while it doesn't have my usual panache, I have a small vial of strychnine, disguised as a tube of lip gloss, shoved inside my jacket pocket. All it would take is uncapping the vial and dumping the contents into his drink and *voila*. I'm another fifty grand richer.

But I'm gunning for the hundred k bonus if I get my hands dirty. So while I could easily eliminate him if he *is* at the Devil's Playground, I have my knife tucked away inside the sheath in my right boot in case I can get him alone first.

He's married, but I'm not worried about that. Winter says that the marriage is on the rocks anyway, and with a coy smile and a crook of my pointer finger, I don't think it would be too difficult to get him to leave with me.

And if I can't, maybe I'll see if that dark-haired guy

with the smirk I bumped into near the bar would like to head back to my hotel instead—

"—and Devil just said to keep our heads up and our guns ready. He has an emergency meeting with Collins tonight. Ten-thirty at the old video store. It's supposed to be about the Snowflakes."

I'm too good at my job to jump when I hear the name of my target—or my current client's affiliation. I don't pause, either, or stumble. I keep moving as though I didn't catch the snippet of their conversation at all—and duck into the empty booth that's right behind them.

I caught a flash of two suited guys leaning back into their seats. A glass is set before each of them, and though they both are covered all the way to their wrists, I'd put fifty down that they're hiding a devil tat somewhere beneath their shirts.

To be fair, I expect a good chunk of the clubbers to be Sinners. This is their turf, the nightclub on their territory, and it's run by one of the top guys in the syndicate. They're untouchable here, and sometimes that makes them cocky and reckless.

Here's hoping this is one of those times.

thou shall not...

THREE
A LEAD

KYLIE

Shifting in my seat so that I'm facing out instead of across the table, I lean forward, sipping my drink, pretending like I'm searching the dance floor when, in reality, I'm doing everything I can to eavesdrop.

From my vantage point, I can see the darker-skinned guy on the farther side of the booth. His hair is cut close to his scalp, his features hard, his eyes darting out into the crowd as he says in a low voice I can barely make out, "Shouldn't he be going to see Harrison?"

"The mayor?" scoffs his companion. "I know you're messing with me, but, shit, no. Everyone knows that Harrison is just a figurehead, Fade. He puts up the front while the vice mayor gets shit done."

Fade snorts. "You mean Harrison fucks those aides of his while Collins runs Springfield."

"Exactly. Harrison likes his twinks. Collins likes his palms greased. The SPD likes their bribes coming, too. As long as the wheels spin, the Sinners profit."

"And we have Devil to thank for it." Fade lifts his drink, leaning forward in his seat. I move my head, acting as though I might've seen who I was looking for off to my left just in time for Fade to clink his glass with the other man. "Cheers, Kill."

"Damn right—"

"Hey. This seat taken?"

Swallowing my annoyance at the interruption, I glance up.

The voice belongs to a guy my age, maybe a little older. He's decent-looking enough. Dark brown hair cut in an expensive style, hazel eyes a little bit glassy. He's not wearing a suit like the guys behind me, but his button-down shirt looks pricey. His top button is undone, giving me a peek at his chest.

He runs his fingers through his hair, lips quirked in an 'I'm harmless' grin. Like he doesn't want to spook me before he gets a chance to actually hit on me.

Normally, I'd let him try. But this is my shot to at least get the closest to my target as I have since arriving in Springfield and, what the hell, why not take it?

And, you never know, maybe I can take *him*.

I've been so bored lately. A bored Kylie inevitably leads to a horny Kylie, and while I have no problem taking care of business myself, it'll be so much easier to borrow a dick for a couple of minutes to get off.

I have some time, though after a second glance, I realize that I'd be wasting it. Considering I can smell the booze on his breath, and those glassy eyes are one of the tell-tale signs he's on Breeze, it's not worth it. The alcohol could leave him with a limp dick, and while Breeze makes you horny, it also turns guys into two-minute men. To satisfy my insatiable lusts, I need more than that.

But it never hurts to have an alibi—or have fun fucking with people.

So instead of telling him to get lost, I shake my head.

Without waiting for an express invitation, he slides into the seat opposite me. His 'harmless' grin becomes a little more predatory as I shift again, moving so that we're facing each other. It gives him a chance to look down my sweater, and he takes it.

Men.

"Hey. Name's Ronnie."

"Beth," I lie.

"I saw you looking around. Thought maybe you were looking for me."

"Maybe I was," I say, twirling the straw in my glass.

When his chest seems to puff up, I know I already have him hook, line, and sinker. "I don't think I've seen you around," he says. "This your first time at the Playground?"

"Yup." Another lie. "I'm from out of town and thought I'd check it out. You?"

"Me? Born and bred in Springfield. As for the Devil's Playground..." Lifting his hand, he rubs the sleeve of his shirt, gesturing to his forearm without ever lifting the fabric up to reveal the flesh beneath. "You could say it's my home away from home."

I'd bet that those other two would be inked with Lincoln 'Devil' Crewes's trademark devil tat. This guy? A Sinner? Not a chance.

But that doesn't mean he can't help me.

Squeezing my arms together, plumping up my cleavage as I lean toward him, I grin. "Really? I'd love to hear more..."

AFTER LEAVING THE DEVIL'S PLAYGROUND, I MAKE A quick stop back at my hotel to ditch my phone and change up my appearance.

Rule number one as a hitwoman? Never bring your phone with you. The way it pings off of the towers tracks you. If I ever got caught and I had my phone with me? They could prove I was nearby when the body went down.

I'll update Winter when I'm done. Until then, I'm off the grid. Just so it's not suspicious, though, I grab the fake ID I sourced for just this hit, plus a couple of bucks in case I need cash. Everything else is hidden in my 'go' bag, including my phone, locked in the hotel room's safe. I left the hotel key behind 'accidentally', knowing I'll just get the front desk to issue me a new one.

I still have the strychnine. The knife. If this goes well, that's all I'll need; if it doesn't end the way I hope it does, at least I should get a little more intel about my target.

Ronnie was no help there. Just like I expected, he didn't know jack shit about the Sinners Syndicate or the politics of Springfield past what I've already figured out for myself. When I would steer the conversation in that direction, I could see right through his lies. Even I knew that Vice Mayor Collins usually meets with Royce 'Rolls' McIntyre—Devil's second, and the manager of the Playground—in order to get his monthly pay-off, while Devil and Damien Libellula have monthly dinners with the actual mayor of Springfield, Hogan Harrison.

So for the Devil of Springfield to be having a quiet meet with the vice mayor? That's unusual, but Ronnie didn't even *know* that the city has a vice mayor.

But you know what he *did* know? Where to find the old video store on the West Side.

He laughed when I mentioned that I heard Springfield still has a place to rent videos somewhere around here. Maybe if I'd visited a good fifteen years earlier, the Blockbuster might have been open, though the empty remains of the big store exist on the edge of downtown Springfield where the hookers and the druggies and the homeless rule the abandoned, rundown quarter.

Dressed like this, I'll stick out like a sore thumb. With a few alterations, my club outfit might help me pass as a prostitute, but I'd rather not attract *that* kind of attention while tracking a target. Instead, I pull my hair back into a messy ponytail, trade my sweater for a plain black t-shirt, and stick with my boots, jeans, and leather jacket. I clean off the face full of evening make-up, going barefaced to sell my 'college student who took a wrong turn' in case the empty side of the city isn't as empty as I expect it to be.

Close to an hour after getting my first lead in almost two weeks, I'm hopping into the ride-share car that I ordered when I was on my way up to my hotel room.

Poor Ronnie. I left my nearly half-full drink on the table, asking him if he wouldn't mind watching it for me while I, ahem, freshened up in the club's bathroom. The way he smacked his lips made it obvious he expected the two of us to head on out somewhere more private after I came back. I wouldn't be surprised if he's still sitting there, waiting for 'Beth' to return.

Nope. The Hummingbird has taken flight, and if all goes well, I'll be migrating out of Springfield by the end of the night.

For now, I book a ride from the hotel out to Mama Maria's, an Italian restaurant in the nicer part of the downtown. They're open until midnight, which would explain my ten o'clock 'reservation', and even better, it's only a straight twelve-block walk away—plus one cross street over—from the area where Vice Mayor Collins is supposed to have his late-night meeting with Lincoln Crewes.

I pay my driver, giving just enough of a tip that he won't remember me for being too cheap or too generous, then skip over to the front door of the restaurant. Once the black car disappears down the street, I take a turn and start heading further downtown.

Within the first six blocks of my walk, bitching into the winter wind as it slaps me in the face, I notice a difference. The traffic all seems to turn off to a street behind me. It's quiet. None of the buildings I'm passing are open, and by the eighth block, they're all obviously closed down or abandoned.

I start to pass some of the unhoused population. Curled up in the empty nooks, buried under blankets to ward off the December chill, none of them peek their heads up to watch me walk by. A pair of sex workers glare at each other from opposite corners, waiting for a john to drive by that doesn't come; at least, not while I'm here.

The redhead on my side loses her sneer as I head past, hands shoved into my jacket pockets.

"You look lost, sweetheart. Don't think this part of Springfield is made for the likes of you."

I give her a grin. "Taking a shortcut to a friend's house," I tell her.

"Shitty friend. They could've picked you up. Met you halfway."

"I'll make sure to tell him that."

She tugs her faux fur jacket closer. Considering how short her black dress is, it's probably the only warmth she has. "Him? Cut your losses there, babe. A real gentleman never would've let you walk through Skid Row at this hour. Stay safe, you hear me?"

I think of the knife in my boot, plus the poison in my pocket. "I will. And good luck tonight."

"It's colder than a witch's tit out," she mutters, more to herself than to me. "At this point, I'll suck a dick for ten bucks just to get into a warm car."

I don't blame her. It's fucking *freezing*. Only the rush of adrenaline I get when I'm stalking a target has my blood pumping; otherwise, I'd be just as cold. For now, the hunt has me fired up, but I mimic her gesture, pulling my jacket closed, and continue on my way to see my 'friend'.

Fingers crossed I find him.

thou shall not...

FOUR
BANG

LUCA

Vice Mayor Collins should've known better than to expect mercy from the Devil of Springfield.

He did, however, know that there was no way to refuse an outright summons from the head of the Sinners Syndicate. When Devil told him to come down to the old Blockbuster, and to come *alone*, the vice mayor listened. The same as how he was ordered to park a street over, leave his phone on the front seat of his car, then meet Devil behind the abandoned, dilapidated video store.

He showed up ten minutes ago. I pulled up outside the Blockbuster closer to twenty, the only car on this stretch of the road. Devil told me to wait, and that's what I've been doing while the boss... based on the first howl of pain I heard shortly after the vice mayor strolled back there, the boss is doing exactly what he's known for.

Devil became a father last summer. Claire is four months old now, and there have been a few rumors that say he's lost his edge since his daughter was born. Yeah, right. He just doesn't put himself into situations where his kid could grow up without a dad. If he thinks anyone is a threat to him... to Springfield... to the Sinners... to Ava and Claire... there is nothing he won't do to put down any threat.

Take Dave Sanders, for example. A fellow Sinner who sold out Cross to Winter and his men, when Cross gave me the heads up that he was working for Winter, I passed the message along to the boss.

When Devil was done with him, Rolls had three garbage bags in the car's trunk, and I used my last liner to keep the bodily fluids from leaking out onto the interior.

You don't betray Devil. Simple as that. You don't threaten his family, and you don't betray the Sinners when you have a devil inked on your skin.

Sometimes, he's quick. Like with Twig. That idiot disrespected Ava in front of the whole syndicate, and Devil shot him in the junk first, then finished him with a headshot. That got the message across. Treat Mrs. Crewes with respect or you'd be next.

Bobby deserved a more brutal death after he sold Devil's wife out to Damien Libellula, but we were on a time crunch for that one. I needed to speed across Springfield so that Devil could confront the head of the Dragonflies and get his wife back. Bobby died, but Devil has his regrets that it was over so quickly.

He got his aggression out with Dave. Taking one of his men, working with an enemy to sell out all of Springfield next... Dave got exactly what he deserved.

And so will the vice mayor.

Devil warned me that he would take as long as he had to to get us as much information out of Collins as he could. If Libellula's information was wrong, if Collins wasn't working with Winter to allow the Snowflakes and their product to infiltrate Springfield, the meet would be a quick one. But if Devil used his proven techniques to get Collins to admit that he *is* on Winter's payroll?

This could take a while.

I'll wait. I'm good at that. The car's got the heat on, and while I usually listen to the radio while I drive, I have the volume on low so that I can hear it if Devil needs me.

So far, so good—

Knock, knock.

Shit.

I jolt at the unexpected rap on my window, one hand dropping to the gun kept in my console, the other landing on the bottom curve of the steering wheel.

I fucked up. Searching for some sign that Devil was

done with the vice mayor, I completely neglected to keep my eye on my surroundings. It's about ten-twenty, ten-thirty on a Thursday night on the far side of Skid Row. Not even the streetwalkers claim this territory—which is why Devil holds meetings just like this one here—and I never expected anyone to come this way after dark.

Especially not *her*.

My heart leaps to my throat when I see the face peering in through my driver's side window.

Fuck, she's *gorgeous*.

That's all I can think about for a split second as I gape like an idiot up at her. Everything about her features is simply stunning. She has this narrow face with enough softness that she seems a little bit younger than I am. It's hard to tell what her complexion is beneath the few-and-far-between lamp-lights, but it reminds me of the color of coffee with a good splash of milk in it. Her hair is a few shades darker; all loose and wild curls barely tamed by her ponytail.

She's smiling at me, gesturing with her fingers for me to roll down my window.

I shouldn't. I know I shouldn't.

I *do*.

"Hi."

Unable to speak just yet, I nod a greeting at her.

She giggles a touch nervously. "So. I've been wandering around for, like, the last twenty minutes or so. My friend told me that he lives down here, just past the old Blockbuster, but here's the Blockbuster, and I don't see anywhere like my friend describes. Then I saw your car and, well... I thought maybe you might know where I'm supposed to go."

I swallow the lump in my throat. "Uh, maybe. Your buddy give you an address?"

She shakes her head, curls bouncing as she does. "I'm terrible when it comes to shit like that. I'm better with landmarks, but he said it's a building with at least twenty floors. I mean, *duh*. His apartment is 20D. But I've gotta be wrong. Maybe there's another Blockbuster that went out of business."

Not that I know of. "Sorry, but doubt it. And all the big apartment buildings start around Sixth. We're on Fourth." Reaching out of the window, I point. "Try heading back that way. It's still close enough, and he's probably over there."

"Yeah. You're right. Thanks for helping. I mean, I'd call him to get better directions, but, stupid me, I left my phone at home."

Take mine.

That's what a good guy would do. Help the damsel in distress, give her my phone to make a quick call—to her friend, or to a car service since she's on foot and I obviously can't offer her a ride—and get her off the dangerous streets of Skid Row at night.

However, I can't—and not just because, as a Sinner on duty, I know better than to get involved with this

51

bubbly beauty. I can't because, suddenly, we're both interrupted by an ear-splitting sound.

Bang.

Bang.

Bang.

Fuck!

The night just exploded with a trio of gunshots. Maybe if it was July, I could play it off like they were fireworks. It's December. Thunder's out, too. That was gunfire, and now the poor girl is staring in terror over the roof of the car.

I don't know what else to do. Hurrying her on before she gets mixed up in Sinners' business seems like the best plan. Before I can even realize what I'm doing, I pop open the door, giving it just enough of a shove that she instinctively takes a few steps away from the town car.

That was an even bigger mistake.

She stumbles closer to the front of the car, eyes still drawn in the direction where the deafening pops just sounded. From that point, it's easy for her to see over the hood right as Devil comes stalking out from behind the empty store, his Sig Sauer still in hand.

"Pop the trunk, Luca," he commands, voice ringing out in the wake of the gunshots' echoes. "Let's get the vice mayor's corpse in the trunk before he makes an even bigger mess on the asphalt."

He didn't see the girl yet. Checking his weapon, barking out orders like usual, he didn't look up the entire time he was telling me what he wanted me to do. If anything, he caught the silhouette against the shadows and thought it was me... but I'm still standing near the open door.

And the girl?

She *books* it.

I don't blame her. Whether she recognizes the boss as the Devil of Springfield or not, he's still a big man in a dark suit, wielding a gun while talking about a corpse. She heard the gunshots. She has to know that Devil just killed someone.

That she runs tells me that she's not as stupid as she thinks she is. She's pretty fucking smart, actually, even if she doesn't have a chance of getting away.

Especially when Devil's head shoots up at the sudden motion. It takes two seconds for it to click, that I wasn't alone, that we have a *witness* before he snaps at me, "Get her!"

I'd expected as much. Whether it's because I've been working for Devil for so long that I know how he thinks or because something about the girl has me unwilling to let her escape me so easily, I don't know. Still, I was already chasing after her before Devil gave me the order to do so.

She's quick, but not quick enough. I run her down, grabbing one hand and tugging her backward so that she slams into my chest.

"No, no, no. Let me go. I... I didn't see anything. You have to let me go!"

I wish I could. Glancing over at the boss, seeing the flat expression on his rugged face as he meets us on the sidewalk, I know that that won't be happening.

A muscle tics in his cheek. "Who is she?"

I wait a beat to see if she'll answer. Give a name or try to continue to talk her way out of what all three of us expect to happen next.

When she doesn't, I shake my head. "Dunno, boss. She said she was lost. Came this way to meet a friend, but got confused. She was asking me for directions when the shots rang out."

"I got as much from Collins as I could," rumbles Devil, face growing ever darker in the shadows. "He was no good for more, so I finished him off."

Ducking her head, trying to hide from us, the girl whimpers.

Moving toward her, Devil grips her chin, jerking her up so that she can't look away.

My stomach flips. Her eyes are big. Wide. *Terrified*.

I want to slap his hand off of her. I don't know where that sudden urge comes from, and I only just manage to keep my hands pinning her arms in place.

Devil runs his dark gaze over her face. Then, without another comment, he marches over to the back of the town car. He finds the unlatch button beneath the trunk, popping it, then shoving it open.

The liner meant for the vice mayor is already laid out. Cross didn't have a tarp on hand, but he gave me four industrial-sized trash bags to protect the car. I'd gotten that ready as soon as Collins appeared, then sat in the driver's seat, waiting for Devil's sign that it was time to go.

The trunk's open. Instead of ordering me to help him heft the vice mayor's dead body into the back, he nods at the girl in my grip.

"Put her in."

Shit. The trunk was for the vice mayor. And while Devil can easily call Rolls and his clean-up crew to take care of Collins after all, I don't see why he has to terrorize the poor girl even further by stowing her in the back like that.

She saw something she wasn't supposed to. Even in a city like Springfield, where the cops are crooked as fuck, bought and paid for, there's a limit to what the local mafias can get away with. Murdering a high-ranking member of the city's government? With a *witness* to the aftermath and Devil's casual discussion of Vice Mayor Collins's dead body?

To make a statement in Springfield—to keep his position of power—Devil has to remind the rest of us just how he earned his nickname. And while he didn't go so far as to use a knife to sever the vice mayor's head from his neck... as far as I know... he ended Collins. Sometimes, bodies have to disappear. Sometimes, they have to be left somewhere obvious to make a bigger impact.

Springfield needed to know that Collins betrayed Devil, and because of that, he paid with his life. But while there would be no doubt that he was the murderer, Devil would never allow there to be *evidence* that could end his reign of power.

And if this girl tells anyone what she saw...

No. She's an innocent. She could be swayed. It doesn't have to be like this.

Thou shall not—

"I said, put her in the trunk, Luca."

Damn it, I put her in the trunk.

IT'S EASIER THAN IT SHOULD BE.

I expected her to resist. To scream. To *fight*. She doesn't do any of that. Despite begging only moments ago for me to release her, the moment that Devil tells me to put her in the trunk, she seems to shut down. It's not even like she goes limp, either, too frightened to do anything but give in. She just lets me maneuver her any way I want until I've tilted her back into my arms before guiding her headfirst into the trunk.

She even helps me by tucking her legs in, and that makes me feel infinitely worse. Like she knows what's coming, that she's resigned to it, and when I meet those big, frightened eyes again, my heart stutters in my chest.

I can't explain it. I've only just met this girl, and part of me wants to risk Devil's wrath by hefting her out of the trunk again and telling her to run.

As it is, I'm surprised that Devil didn't just fire off another round when he realized there was a witness. The man I first started working for would have, but as brutal as he could be then, that's nothing compared to how a man acts when he has something to lose.

He has a wife to protect. A baby to protect. A syndicate to lead... and enemies coming at us from all sides.

Devil won't just shoot first anymore. He has questions, and he uses his methods to get answers. I know that's what he was doing behind Blockbuster before he finished the vice mayor off. Getting the politician to spill his guts about what he did for Winter, then blowing him away when he was done.

Is that what he plans for this poor girl? Find out what she saw, then she'll become just another casualty? Collateral damage of the wars between the Sinners and our enemies?

I know what kind of man Devil is. I begged him to let me work for him for just that reason. I might not be a killer myself, but I respect how far the boss will go to keep the Sinners safe and in power. Snitches get stitches. Traitors die.

But pretty girls who got lost and saw something they weren't meant to?

I can't let her go. As much as I want to, to disobey Devil is as much of a death sentence as meddling in mafia biz. But that doesn't mean I can't figure out a way to keep the boss happy *and* help the brunette in the trunk get out of this mess.

I dip my hand into my jacket pocket, searching for the small vial I never leave home without.

Unlike most of my fellow Sinners, I don't carry a piece on me. Even those of us who don't serve as enforcers or handle clean-up for Devil are often armed. That's kind of our thing. The Sinners Syndicate runs the guns and weapon trade in the city, and keeping a gun on our hip is as much advertising as it is practicality in this line of work.

Like how Rolls has his Beretta, and even Cross carries, but the mafia fixer and artist rarely fire them. I technically have a Ruger for protection—Devil insists —but I keep it in the town car most of the time, only relocating it to my personal vehicle when I have a rare day to myself.

The vial, though? That's more my speed, and something I've hung onto since I volunteered to infiltrate Winter's holding facility in Hamilton to rescue Cross. Tanner gave me one of the knock-out drugs our tech guy had perfected for Mace Burns a year or two back. I couldn't risk bringing my Ruger, but if my cover was blown, I could jab one of the other hired goons with the injector and hope it knocked them out so I could make my escape.

I kept it after we were all back in Springfield again. I doubted that Winter would come after me once he realized I was working for the Sinners all along. Just in case, it seemed like a good idea to hold onto the drug for an easy out without having to worry about adding the ninth tally mark to my tat.

Did I ever think I'd use it on a young woman in the trunk of Devil's town car? Fuck, no. But as she watches me, lips working though she doesn't say anything I can make out over the beat of my heart, I use my thumb to flip off the cap.

Palming the small vial, I reach into the trunk. I lay my fingers on top of her hair—soft, it's so springy and goddamn *soft*—my heart doing a little jump when she doesn't try to yank herself away from my touch.

I give her a crooked grin full of promise. "Everything will be okay," I tell her before shifting my hand so that the needle is hovering over her skin.

And then I jab it.

thou shall not...

FIVE
OFFICER BURNS

LUCA

"**W**hat are you— *ow*!"

My stomach twists at her cry of pain, but what else can I do? I'd rather her be blissfully unaware of what happens next. Whether it's a ride in the trunk or... or whatever Devil has planned for her, it's the least I can do.

Or is it?

Before I can see the renewed look of fear and terror and hurt in her big, brown eyes, I firm my resolve and grab the lid of the trunk. I feel the shake of its slam all the way to my bones as it shuts, and only hope there's enough oxygen in there to keep her breathing.

Devil is already in the back seat by the time I'm sliding into mine behind the wheel. With the engine on, I shift the car into drive and peel off down the empty street.

I don't say anything for the first few minutes of the drive. My thoughts are with the girl in the trunk and how I laid her out on trash bags meant for a bloody body. I haven't prayed in years, but I find myself muttering 'Our father...' under my breath as I sneak a peek in the rearview mirror.

Any car that I use to drive Devil around comes with a glass divider. I prefer it. There are certain elements of the business that I was uncomfortable with at first. I didn't need to hear the details of how the girls upstairs are trained and treated—especially when more than a couple of them offered me a freebie once they realized how screwed-up I am—or where and when a gun drop-off would be happening. He's the boss. I'm the driver. I've earned his trust, and I did that by insisting on keeping that divider up.

We both have a control to lower it. If Devil has directions for me or other orders, he can drop the divider so that he doesn't have to raise his voice. In the three years that I've been his driver, I've never used the control on the dash.

Until now.

I don't know what comes over me. I can see that he has his phone up to his ear; from the shape, style, and color on the back, I know it's the phone he uses for business, not the one that is devoted solely to his wife's calls.

I clear my throat, catching his attention. "Boss?"

"Hang on, Royce." Devil lowers his phone. "What is it, Luca?"

I drop my gaze from the rearview mirror, staring out through the windshield instead so that I can't see the boss's reflection as I ask him plainly, "Can I have her?"

I don't have to say who.

Devil sucks in a breath. "What do you mean? You wanna keep her?"

Yes.

What?

"No. Not like that. Not like—"

"You mean, not like Devil who blackmailed his wife into marrying him so that I could keep my Ava?"

There's a dangerous edge to his voice when he reminds us of his first wedding to his wife. Most of the Sinners don't know the true story of how Devil convinced his wife to marry him for that first time. Their second wedding was a syndicate affair; after a large church wedding, they even had a reception at the Devil's Playground that we all attended. But their first wedding is an open secret in his inner circle— including the driver who sometimes hears more than he should.

It worked out for him. Ava Crewes is head over heels for Devil, and the mother of his child. She would do anything for him...

...and, suddenly, I have an idea.

"Let me keep her, boss. Let me make her mine. If I win her heart... if I win her loyalty... she won't snitch."

"A dead girl won't snitch, either," Devil says. "I'm sorry, Luca, but facts are facts. The DA's salivating over someone who's willing to talk. You know how many Sinners and Dragonflies we've had to disappear because they were willing to turn state's witness against me and Damien? Fuck, no. Especially with Winter close enough to buy off Collins, we can't dick around. The girl has to go."

My fingers flex around the steering wheel. I dare a peek in the rearview mirror. "What if I take responsibility for her? Make it so she won't blab?"

"She's a liability."

"She doesn't have to be."

For a moment, Devil stares into my soul, dark eyes meeting mine in the reflective surface... and then he lifts the phone back to his ear. "Royce? Yeah. Take care of Collins for me." A pause. "No. Don't worry about the girl yet. I'm still making up my mind on that. Yeah." Another pause. "Right. Call you back. Oh, and tell Nicolette sorry for pulling you out of bed. If it makes you feel any better, me and Luca won't be turning in anytime soon, either. Bye."

Devil drops the phone against his meaty thigh. ""Go on. Tell me what you're thinking."

I don't even know *what* I'm thinking, only that those pretty brown eyes of hers have seared their way into my brain. But I try my best as I navigate the streets that have become as much a part of me as the blood in my veins. All of my attention is back on the road even as my thoughts are with the girl in the trunk—*Is she okay? Did the sedative take? Will she* hate *me...*—as I make my case.

Devil lets me ramble as we roll. When I'm done, all he does is lift his phone back up again after selecting a contact.

I wait, heart beating wildly in my chest.

"Burns? It's Devil. I need a favor..."

Tanner explained that, once injected with the sedative, the effects would last for about four hours. Depending on the height and weight of the person I used it on, it could be a little longer, a little shorter.

Banking on the fact that I should have at least the four hours—though, realistically, it would be longer since the girl in the trunk is smaller than a full-grown man—I didn't waste any time.

Officer Mason Burns—Mace for short, though most of us just refer to him as Burns—is a cop on Devil's payroll. About a decade older than me, give or take, he's been a beat cop his entire career. He likes it that way, too, walking around the city, patrolling with his new trainee, and reporting back to Devil for a hefty deposit to his bank account at the end of the month.

He's not the only cop that Devil pays for. At least

one-third of the Springfield PD is bought by the Sinners Syndicate, with another chunk serving on Damien Libellula's dime. But when I asked Devil if I could have the girl, he immediately got in touch with Burns.

On the one hand, Rolls and Devil agreed that the vice mayor's body needed to be found. If only to remind the rest of Springfield not to even think about rising up against the Sinners, he needed to be made an example of. Plus, the battered, bloody, and bullet hole-riddled corpse would be a message to Johnny Winter, too.

Rolls, Killian, and Juan are responsible for relocating the body away from the scene. A heads up to Burns and his fellow officers—including his lieutenant —meant the murder would be a 'tragedy', but not necessarily a crime. Some of the straight cops might try to investigate it as such. They won't get too far, and with Mayor Harrison desperate to keep his secret about fucking male aides half his age while presenting himself as a happily married, doting Christian father of four, he'll have a new vice mayor by the end of the week, no questions asked about what exactly happened to the last one.

That's the thing. Without someone reputable to admit they saw what happened, it's easy to get away with murder. A bubbly girl at the wrong place at the wrong time could be the Sinners' downfall if the right cop or the right judge took up the case.

Maybe we could buy her off. Everyone in Springfield has a price, and it's possible that Devil could've found hers. Then again, maybe it would just be easier to make her disappear. Walking around Skid Row alone after dark... wasn't she just asking for trouble?

That's how Devil sees it.

Not me.

I've never thought of myself as a white knight before, but something about her... I know we only had one conversation, but even before she opened her mouth, I was struck dumb by her beauty. I haven't felt such instant attraction to anyone since Emily, and there are times I remember her and wonder if I wanted her so badly because she was Emily or because she was the only girl my age in the HCofJD.

Devil doesn't say it, but I get the vibe that he only agreed to give me the girl because it's the first time I've shown any interest in one since I've been a Sinner. I try not to look too closely at that. If he's telling me I can basically babysit our captive until the vice mayor sitch is all taken care of, or I can convince her to keep quiet, I'm not going to second-guess it.

I'll do anything to keep her from becoming another casualty.

Should I be so enthralled by a woman I barely met? Of course not. But I blame myself. If she hadn't knocked on my window... if I hadn't been parked on the street, waiting for the boss... if her pouty lips and bright eyes and wild curls hadn't distracted me... she wouldn't be sprawled out on a cot in Mace Burns's basement.

That's exactly where we are. In a small mountain town about an hour and a half outside of Springfield, Officer Burns owns a wooden hunting cabin that he uses to flee the big city with his wife. Devil knew about it, and the favor he asked of the cop? Was to let me bring the girl in the trunk up to the mountains where I'll keep her with me until everything blows over—or Devil has to make another decision.

He doesn't *need* a driver. He's perfectly capable of driving himself around, and if he wants to keep up appearances, he can just grab one of the other Sinners while I'm out of town. Without any family that I'm in contact with, it's not like I need to be around for the holidays, either. If I want the girl, I have to keep the girl, and that means as my prisoner in a bonafide cop's secret basement.

There's a cot down here. A shower and a toilet down here. A lock on the basement door and—more importantly—the cot comes equipped with a pair of handcuffs looped around the headboard bars, plus chains perfect for what Devil has in mind: well and truly making this girl my prisoner until I can make her my... my...

Fuck if I know what she's going to be. But I've made myself her protector, and that's what I'm going to do.

It's been three hours now. That's how long it took for Burns to meet us at the Playground to drop off his keys, then for me to drop Devil off at Paradise Suites before I stopped at my place to pack whatever shit I thought I'd need for a while. I was taking the town car with me—obviously, considering the precious cargo in the trunk—and with Burns's address plugged into the GPS on the dash, I started the ninety-minute drive a little past midnight.

Burns doesn't have any neighbors. His cabin is at the end of a long, winding, dirt path, surrounded by trees. I parked the town car behind it to be on the safe side, and after opening up the cabin, turning the lights on, and finding the door that leads to the basement, I went and retrieved the girl.

Devil already searched her over. She has no ID so, for now, she's just the girl in the trunk. She told me she left her phone at home, and she must've because she doesn't have one of those, either. In fact, the only thing we found was a tube of lip gloss and some cash.

She's still sleeping now, wearing the leather jacket she had on and a pair of black winter boots. I leave them on as I lay her out on the bed. Seeing the hand-cuffs, knowing I have to even if I don't *want* to, I reach for her nearest hand.

Her nails are short and manicured, the pink polish impeccable. No rings on her fingers—and, yes, I looked purposely—though I do see that she has a faded tattoo peeking out from between her thumb and forefinger.

It's an 'H'. Drawn in a vaguely cursive style, that's all it is. An 'H'.

I wonder what it means?

I run my thumb over the web of her hand, absently tracing the inked 'H' hidden there when her hand is closed. Her skin is so soft, I can't stop myself from fantasizing about what it would be like if *she* was touching *me*.

Stroking me.

Fondling me...

Fuck.

What are you doing, Luca? She's at your mercy. You brought her here to keep her safe, not to fantasize about shit that will never, ever happen.

I need her loyalty. That's it. If that means I need to steal her love, too, I will. To keep her alive, she has to want to protect me and my fellow Sinners above all else. If I expect that she'll go running to the cops first chance she gets, Devil won't even be the one to put her down. It'll be my responsibility.

She is my responsibility.

And the first thing I have to do is make sure that she can't leave me before I can convince her that she wants to keep quiet about what she saw...

Holding her arm over her head, laying it on the pillow, I use the free side of the handcuff attached to the headboard to keep her on the bed. She's motionless and still, the sedative holding her under as I quickly drop to my knee.

Trying not to think about what Burns and his wife do down here with a pair of handcuffs and a shackle and length of chain connected to one of the cot's legs, I fish it out from under the bed. It's sturdier than the cuffs, and because it's heavy, too, I make sure to loop the metal shackle over the top of her jeans to protect her ankle.

There. One hand cuffed to the headboard, a leg chained to the cot. She'll stay right where I put her until I can explain why I had to take her. I don't want to hurt her. I've basically kidnapped her to keep her safe, but despite the naivety she gave off earlier tonight— walking around Skid Row without her phone, for one —I don't think she's going to be happy to wake up and realize she's trapped in this mountain cabin with me.

She will be. I'll make her love me. I'll do whatever it takes so that this innocent creature will never betray me. I'll be her captor and her savior, and when I'm sure that I own her completely, I'll let her go somewhere far away from Springfield, where she can be safe and Devil won't consider her a threat to squeal on us.

Crouching low, I trail my fingers across her forehead, stroking the top of her hair.

God, she's so fucking beautiful. I only wish that we'd met in a different life, or in a different way. Before my parents fucked me up, or Emily shattered my heart to the point it's basically unusable. Before she was there in the aftermath of Devil killing Collins. Before she ran and I had to chase her...

I might have been able to love her. Already, I feel a kinship with this woman. Like I was meant to rescue her, and she was meant to stumble into my life if only so I could protect hers. I'm finding it difficult to refrain from touching her. Even now, I'm caressing her skin before brushing her curls out of her face so that I can marvel at the length of her eyelashes, or how her lips curve slightly even as she's unconscious.

I might have been able to love her, but I won't be able to set her free until I'm sure she trusts me. It's the only way I can trust *her*. And then she can return to her life, I'll go back to my steering wheel, and we can both forget any of this happened.

Because, if we don't, she's dead.

And as loyal as I am to the boss, I just... I can't let that happen.

SIX
FUN

KYLIE

Wow. There's nothing like coming to, groggy and dry-mouthed, fucking *chained* to a cot to make you realize that you lost your edge.

They got me. Not like I made it that hard. I saw the Sig Sauer in Devil's massive paw. If the driver didn't grab me as quickly as he did, I have no doubt in my mind that the head Sinner would've shot me down to get me to stop.

To be honest, I'm still kind of surprised that he didn't. From all the research I did on the mafias that run Springfield, everything I learned made me sure that he wouldn't hesitate to kill.

But I'm alive. My head feels like it weighs a hundred pounds. My mouth tastes like I tasted a shag carpet from a 1970s living room. My arms ache, and my legs... my legs...

I blink.

Okay. My right leg has some kind of metal shackle on it. The shackle itself is attached to a length of chain that slinks off the edge of the narrow cot I'm sprawled out on. And the chain is—

Oh. No wonder my arms ache. Not both, I notice, now that I'm slowly becoming more coherent. But while my right leg has a shackle on it, my left arm is stretched over my head. One half of a pair of handcuffs is encircled on my wrist. The other? Looped around one of the bars on the headboard.

What the fuck?

I can't see what's going on with the chain because my arm is stuck. I don't like that. Whatever kinky shit is going on here, I'm not about to stay put on this bed, waiting for my captor to return.

Who did this? The Devil of Springfield? The chauffeur who answered my knock on his window? It can't be Walt Collins since I distinctly remember hearing the gunshots that rang out, obviously ending his life before anyone else had the chance to kill the shady vice mayor. But when I was convinced that I was next, what the hell happened that I ended up...

Where?

I glance around. I have no idea where the fuck I am. I get 'basement' vibes, from the chill down here to the cement floor and the stairs across the room that lead to another level, but it's December. For all I know, I'm in some weirdo's bedroom or garage. Either way, I'm stuck, and considering the last thing I remember, that's probably not a good thing.

Well, fuck me. That's what a dash of boredom, a pinch of recklessness, and a hint of a death wish get you. I screwed up, and while I was almost welcoming the bullet I expected between my eyes for getting snagged by the Devil of Springfield and one of his goons, they made a mistake, too.

They took me alive.

I take another gander around, getting a better lock on my surroundings.

There's a mini fridge that I'm pretty sure is plugged in based on the slight hum I'm picking up on. A long, narrow table about a foot high in the middle of the space. A waste basket. A door that's closed, and not a single window. Luckily, there is a single high-watt light bulb in the center of the room, helping me see everything down here. Otherwise I'd be sitting in the darkness, judging my life choices.

No. I'm just doing that at the blinding light on overhead, causing me to squint.

Ugh. I know I've been in a rut lately. I've been chasing the same high I got when I took my first life, and after a decade, it's lost its luster. I'll admit it. I've been going through the motions. Even the prospect of a high-profile hit wasn't enough to really rev my engine. That was why I jumped at the chance to finish it all off tonight if I could. I'd beat the Christmas deadline, get the money owed to me by Winter, and find something else to give me that same sense of satisfaction and enjoyment.

I actually experienced a spark of it tonight. For the first time in a loooong time, when I rapped on that window and the man inside jumped like a frightened rabbit, I had to bite the inside of my cheek to keep from laughing.

That wouldn't have fit the image I was trying to put on. Neither would the outright flirting I wanted to do when I got my first look at him. He was better looking than I was expecting from the profile, and if he hadn't been sitting in the expensive, shiny black car idling outside of the Blockbuster, I might have flirted with him after all.

The car had to belong to the Devil of Springfield. I'd heard about how he has a personal driver to ferry him around the city. Why? No idea, but even if it *wasn't* Devil's car, there had to have been a reason it was the only visible car on the stretch of road where Crewes and Collins were supposed to meet.

Unless, you know, those two guys at the Playground got it wrong. It could've been a drug deal taking place around back, or one of the girls the street over found a willing buyer after all. I didn't know, but without going around back myself, I had no idea.

The direction I headed down the street meant I couldn't do that unless I wheeled back around. I could've, but something about the driver waiting in the car had me going with my first idea.

Up until the moment I knocked, I planned on just walking by as if I had every right to be there. I couldn't get to my target with others around anyway, and Winter only paid me for one head, not three. I certainly wasn't going to eliminate the vice mayor, the mafia leader, and his driver on *one* commission which meant my entire trek down Skid Row was a colossal waste of time.

And yet... I'd never turn down the chance to get some intel. Even if it was cementing my story for why I was there, then moving on, I was going to do it.

I just never expected that Lincoln Crewes would blow away Vice Mayor Collins when I was right fucking there—or that he would set eyes on me after the fact before I could pull a rabbit.

To be fair, until his gaze landed on me, I did think I had a bit of a death wish. When that murderous gaze found me in the dark and the cold, I realized just how much I wanted to survive when my first instinct was to bolt.

The driver guy caught me, though. He dropped me in the trunk like Devil told him to, and I played the part of a good little girl, letting him think I was under his complete control while plotting how I was going to escape the trunk before they got me to a second location.

That's self-preservation 101. Never let them take you to a second location, and I wasn't planning on it.

Too bad I didn't plan on the driver injecting me with something that had me knocked out within minutes...

How long was I out? No idea. Long enough that someone was able to bring me here, truss me up, and I was unconscious through all of it.

I'm not anymore. I'm wide awake now, and my focus is on getting out of this bed first, then out of this unfamiliar room second.

Focusing on the handcuff to start, I give my wrist an experimental twist. Whoever clasped in on me was careful not to tighten it too much. I'm confident that I can slide my hand out with only a couple of scrapes around the widest part of my hand, but before I attempt to do that, I notice something about the cuffs.

They're cheap. Chintzy. Unless I'm wrong, they're fucking *toys*.

And my captor only had a single pair to trap one of my hands. That means my right hand is free to do whatever I need it to.

Dumbass. Considering a majority of the population is right-handed, he could've made it a lot harder on me by cuffing that one instead of my left. He didn't, though, and I quickly use my dominant hand to unclasp the back of my silver hoop earring.

I've worn the same pair of earrings since my mom and dad gave them to me as an eighth-grade graduation present. They're comfortable, work well with my style, and when I need something a little sharp and pointy in a pinch, they do the job.

I need a little more effort to twist my body and my head so that I can get a better look at the handcuffs. What I see proves my initial suspicion correct. These are shitty cuffs. You don't even need a key to remove them. A pin—or the back of an earring—is enough to trigger the locking mechanism on cuffs like these.

It takes a few frustrating minutes to get the earring in the hole while only being able to use my one hand, but I'm determined. I don't want to catch the attention of my captor, either—assuming he's somewhere nearby—so when I manage to pop the lock, I swallow my cry of, "Fuck yeah," as best I can before turning my attention to the chains.

Here's hoping that the same cheapskate didn't bother with actual chains.

Makes sense. Most people who get nabbed by the mafia would probably be contained by garbage chains and toy handcuffs; it's more their own fears that would keep them captive than anything their abductors used to keep them trapped.

But Kylie Ferguson isn't *most* people. Contrary by nature—and more than a little prone to amuse and challenge myself however I can—if whoever stole me wants me on the bed, I'm getting up, one way or another.

The handcuffs were easy. The length of chain?

Not so much.

The shackle is stuck. The heavy chains are unbreakable. I nearly bend my earring, trying to see if I can pick the lock on the shackle before giving up on that and replacing the earring in my ear.

That doesn't stop me, though. There has to be a way to break free of the chains, and I'm going to find it. If I have to break the leg on the cot that it's attached to, or—

Hang on. Crawling to the bottom of the cot so that I can get a better look at the chains, I feel like an idiot that I focused on the shackled end of the chains for as long as I did. The other side has to be connected to something else to keep me on the bed, and I snort under my breath when I realize just how tiny the metal loop is that keeps the chains connected to the cot by one of its legs.

I kick it. I know I'm risking the noise traveling upstairs, catching the attention of my captor, but I don't care. Using the boots I'm still wearing, I kick and I kick, and when the metal loop starts to buckle under the force of my strike, I kick again until it completely breaks away from its weak solder.

I'm still wearing a shackle. The length of chain trails behind it like a snake. Doesn't matter. I can get up and walk around now with nothing stopping me.

Once I'm on my feet, I do a quick rundown on myself.

Boots? Check. Leather jacket? Check. The curls in

my ponytail are smashed flat—from my time in that stupid trunk, or how I was lying passed out on the cot —but apart from the lingering nasty taste in my mouth and the fuzzy headache that's still kicking my ass, I'm okay.

Well. Okay-*ish*.

I don't have my knife, but I already knew that. Whatever shit he gave me, I had enough brains to ditch the knife before they could use it on me. Same thing with the bluish hummingbird crystal I kept in my pocket. I planned to leave it behind with the body if I managed to off my target, but when that all went to hell, I didn't want to get caught with my signature crystal on me.

Fucking Springfield. I don't know if the one I left behind at the tattoo shop was ever found or, if it was, they managed to link the arson to an assassination attempt made by the infamous Hummingbird, but it was bad enough I got snagged by Devil and his henchman. Having my cover blown at the same time would be like rubbing salt inside a wound.

Patting my jacket, I snort when I feel the lip gloss-shaped lump. I have no illusion that whoever put me here wouldn't have gone through my pockets before they trussed me up like that. Just as I expected, they completely disregarded the lip gloss as something a silly girl kept in her pocket.

Good. I can use that.

And if necessary, I can use the strychnine, too.

That perks me up. Someone went to a lot of trouble to keep me alive. They want me as their prisoner for some reason, and if I acquiesced as easily as I did earlier tonight, that's only because I didn't plan on being their prisoner for long.

I still don't, but with this in my pocket, it's my ace in the hole—and a way to get out of this before I really do become the next victim.

Do I think I will? Not really. I'm here for a reason, but now that I'm awake, I'm not going to sit down here and wait to find out what it is. That's not my style, and if someone else is here with me, I'd much prefer to throw them off-guard by being like nothing they expect.

I always do.

Another sweep, looking for something that I can use as a weapon if necessary. The closest thing I have is the chain rattling against the floor with every step I take. Dropping low, I grab the end of it. It's not really long enough to hurt someone, but if I have to hear the scrape as I head up the stairs, I'll lose it.

Because the stairs? That's exactly where I'm going.

My plan is to bang on the door so that, if someone *is* up there, they know they have a conscious, cranky captive on their hands. Despite the cuff and chains being overkill for little ol' me, I honestly expected that the door at the top would be locked.

It isn't.

Huh.

The doorknob turns easily under my hand. I mean, I had to check, and I blink a few times in rapid succession when it opens. I ease the door out as slowly as possible, waiting for a gun or a knife or a scarred brawler with a scowl and dark, cruel eyes to appear in the gap.

Am I being held by the Devil of Springfield? I don't know, but after how he glowered at me, I'd rather take my chances with anyone else.

Is this my bid to escape? Not really. Call me a glutton for punishment, but this is the most excitement I've had in months. Witnessing a murder that I didn't perform? Being tossed in a trunk? Tied up in what I'm more and more sure is a basement only God knows where?

I'm having a blast now that I'm not dead!

So, that thought in mind, I say 'fuck it' and use my palm to shove the door open all the way.

Whoops. I used a little more force than I should've because the answering slam of my hand against the wood fills the room I'm peering into.

I'm not alone. To my right, I see a man. His arms are stretched out on the top of the two-seater couch, legs spread as his head is tilted back, eyes closed, lips slightly parted. Unless I was imagining it, he was snoring, too, though that stops as soon as his eyes snap open.

I know who he is. I saw that surprisingly handsome face earlier tonight. Those shocking green eyes. The sandy brown hair seemingly sticking up in random places.

It's the driver who drugged me.

He jumps to his feet, pointing at my chest. "What are you... *how* did you... what?"

Releasing my hold on the lip gloss container in my pocket, I jerk my thumb behind me. "You forgot to lock me down there."

His mouth falls open all the rest of the way, the heights of his chiseled cheeks turning a slight shade of pink.

Without another word, he slowly—almost sheepishly—sidles over to the front door. A *snick*-ing sound later, that door is locked, too.

I smile.

You know what? This is gonna be *fun*.

thou shall not...

SEVEN
LUCA

KYLIE

I t takes him a moment to recover. To accept that I'm really there, and that while it's true he neglected to lock the door to keep me downstairs, the reason I shouldn't be upstairs at all is hanging loosely from my grip as I walk toward the nearest window and peek outside.

One look and I confirm my suspicion that I'm not in Springfield any longer. It's a big city with multiple sectors, but despite the urban, suburban, and crowded downtown areas, there's one thing that it's missing: mountains and trees.

What do I see outside the window?

Mountains.

And trees.

There's more snow up here, too. I can see it

weighing down the empty branches, piling up on the dirt path. It must be from an older storm since the fresh tire tracks drove right through the unplowed side yard, allowing me to see the frozen dirt beneath it.

From when he drove me up here? Probably.

But why?

I thought I'd get a bullet in the back of my head. Instead, I'm in a small house, cabin-type thing, up on a snowy mountain at Christmas, with a good-looking guy who is holding a decidedly un-mafia-like weapon as though he's never carried before.

Revolver, obviously. Another glance clocks it as a .22 caliber. Guns aren't my weapon of choice—not when they're so fucking *easy*—but I know my snub-nosed revolvers. Mainly because they're some of the most common types of concealed carry, and I need to know if my targets are hiding weapons on them, but either way, I'm pretty sure he has a Ruger LCR.

He's pointing it down. I swallow my snort. Amateur. In my line of work, you learn quickly that, if you're holding a gun, you better be prepared to use it. Pointing it at the floor? What is he going to do? Shoot straight into the basement while I'm standing by the window?

Please. I could disarm him and have him kissing his own gun in less than ten seconds if he's going to keep it at his side like that.

Even better, he has no idea.

His forehead is furrowed into thick lines. The dark

circles under his eyes seem to shadow them, darkening the shade of his green irises. He probably only just dozed off when my sudden appearance woke his ass up. Me, on the other hand? I've been out for a good six or seven hours, considering it's not dark outside any longer. It's morning, and it's time to face what today will bring.

It takes him a few moments to recover, but it takes me even longer to realize that he's staring at me like that because he doesn't know what to make of me. And while I often have that effect on people, in this situation, I'm doing what I wanted to do: acting nothing like he probably expected me to.

The driver looks like he thought I would start sobbing in terror. At the very least, I should be freaking out. Right? Maybe demanding to know where I am, what's going on, and what he's going to do with me... but I didn't.

Oopsie.

Is it too late to conjure a tear or two to really throw him off?

Ah, well. I shake the chain. "Since these didn't do shit, you think you can take them off?"

While he just gapes at me, I give him a once-over. I'm pretty sure he was wearing a black jacket before. A suit jacket? He's a mafia guy so probably. He has on a long-sleeved button-down shirt, a pair of black suit pants, and matching black sneakers. The shirt fits him well. Not only does it show off his long, lean build, but

I notice a tiny silver key is hanging off of a thin chain looped around his slender neck.

I point at it. "Is that the key? Please. This is just annoying."

Instead of reaching up for the necklace, he dips his hand into his pants pocket. He pulls out three sets of keys: one smaller than the key hanging off his neck, one a little larger, and a car key.

He selects the second key, disappears the others, then walks over to me.

So the one on his neck isn't for the chains. For the handcuffs, then? Or is that the smaller one he pulled out of his pocket?

And if it is, why is he wearing a key around his neck?

I want to know, but I want this stupid shackle off me more so I just stick out my boot and wait.

Without a word, he bends down, jamming the key into the shackle. He wiggles it around, the shackle pops open, and I let the links hit the floor.

I could use my elbow to power-drive him right next to the chains. Before he even face-planted, it would be child's play to snatch his gun out of his waistband and shoot him with his own bullets. That gun holds eight rounds. I'd only need one to kill him.

Only... I don't want to. Not yet, at least.

Not until I know what exactly is going on.

As if he finally realizes that I'm still out of the loop, he lifts his head so that he can look at me. His eyes search my face, and when he's done, he pushes his body easily from the floor. His hands are empty again as he holds them up, as though showing me he's unarmed and harmless now that he tucked his gun away.

Let's see him shoot himself in the ass. 'Cause that'll be even *more* fun...

"Okay. Let's get the obvious out of the way," he says, and I'm momentarily struck by how warm and soothing his voice is. At first glimpse, I thought he might actually be a year or two younger than me. Hearing his voice from outside of the car, I adjust that to him actually being a little *older*. Twenty-seven, maybe, or twenty-eight. He has a bit of a baby face about him, like me, but that's a man's voice, and I respond to it more than I should. "Devil just needs your word that you won't squeal. Okay? You didn't see anything."

Oh. Right. I got myself captured by a mafia man because I happened to be there right as his boss blew away one of the most powerful politicians in Springfield.

I figured that's what happened. And now he wants me to believe that all I have to do is cross my heart, hope to die, stick a needle in my eye-pinkie promise that I'll be a good girl and keep my mouth shut about what I saw?

Where would the fun be in that?

Poor guy. He has to know that it would never be

that easy. Why else has he gone to all this trouble to relocate me to the fucking *mountains* if the first impression I gave him was of someone who would snitch the second he could?

I mean, what kind of innocent bystander would I be if I didn't let him be the big, bad villain he wants me to think he is?

Now, I don't know what his deal is. Not really. However, I'm a pro at reading people. Always have been. One look at Lincoln Crewes and I knew he'd kill me, then step over my corpse if I collapsed in his path.

But his driver? He's different.

When I look at him, I'm not looking at a killer—but he currently is when he looks at *me* imploringly like that.

Hell. Already I can think of three ways to incapacitate him, then eliminate him. The fireplace isn't on, but there's a fire poker propped on top of the mantel. He'd never expect me to attack him, so if I dove for his knees, I could probably get him on his back with the chain wrapped around his throat before he even knew it. That flower planter on the small table by the window looks heavy enough to brain someone.

And that's not counting what a dose of strychnine could do...

He doesn't see a killer, though. He seems a victim.

For now, I'll give him one.

I bat my lashes, giving my foot an experimental shake now that the chains are off. I didn't realize how much it all weighed until the shackle was gone, and remembering how I felt when I first woke up to discover it on me, I look over at him and say, "A good citizen would report she was a witness to a murder. She'd go straight to the cops."

"There are no good citizens in Springfield," he responds. "No good cops, either."

Well... he's not wrong about that. But does that stop me from arguing his point?

Nope.

"Of course there are," I lie.

His expression turns slightly apologetic. "In that case, it looks like you'll be staying here with me until you give me a different answer."

Yup. Figured that out, too. Not that it was hard. The cuffs and the chains were pretty much a neon sign that said 'sit down and stay a while'.

No wonder why he's still gauging my mood after his pronouncement. He basically just admitted his intention of locking me in this cabin of his after abducting me in Springfield, all to protect his boss. I should be pleading for my freedom, not shrugging and acting like I couldn't care less.

I know why he's surprised. Earlier, I played the innocent, air-headed ingenue as I babbled at him, trying to distract him long enough to get an idea of where Devil and Collins were, and what exactly was going on behind the Blockbuster.

I blame Ronnie. Guy wanted to get his dick wet so

badly, he interrupted me while I was eavesdropping on those two Sinners. I heard enough to know that the Devil of Springfield and the vice mayor were meeting up, but I had no idea that it was an ambush—or that only one of those men was walking away from it alive.

Now that I'm here, I see no reason to keep up the act. He stole Kylie.

He gets Kylie.

Only... he has no idea that I *am* Kylie, and he proves that when the next question out of his mouth is:

"What's your name?"

Does he honestly believe I'm going to tell him that?

There's a reason why I left any and all ways to identify me back at the hotel. It sucks that my phone's there, too, but at least I was smart enough to ditch the fake ID on me before I approached the shiny black town car. Even if one of the Sinners goes back to sweep the area, the most they'll find is a counterfeit New York State driver's license with my picture and the name Beth Maroney on it.

When it hits him that I'm not going to answer him, he frowns. "You don't know your name?"

"Oh. I do. But I'm not letting *you* know what it is."

The frown cuts a deep line into his handsome features. "Why not?"

I shrug. "You have to work for it."

Again, probably not what he was expecting from the chick he met earlier tonight, but the sooner he understands that I'm not going to be as easy to control as he thinks, the better.

He wants me here? As long as he doesn't actually try to point that gun in my direction, I'm okay with that. I'll stick around, see exactly what he plans to do with me before I decide what to do with *him*, but it definitely won't be *easy*.

Poor guy. He doesn't get that.

Yet.

He pauses for e moment, then pulls a lazy smile to his face. Damn, he's even more adorable now… "My name is Michael. You can call me Mike, if you want."

My lips twitch. "You're cute, but you're also lying."

His smile falters. "What?"

I purposely make my voice as low as I can, mimicking Lincoln Crewes's deep voice. "'Put her in the trunk, Luca'." I switch back to mine as I say sweetly, "That ring any bells?"

I wait a beat, a smirk tugging on my lips.

"*Luca.*"

thou shall not...

EIGHT
BABYSITTER

KYLIE

"Fuck. You heard that?"

Oh, yeah. I did.

"Delayed reaction on whatever you gave me, I guess. I had a good five minutes after to panic wildly before I blissfully went under. Thanks for that."

Luca has the decency to be a little ashamed. "I was trying to keep you calm."

"Before that other guy killed me?"

And there it is. I just put it out there—and he doesn't deny it.

Instead, he says, "I got the boss to let me watch over you. To explain why it's in your best interest to keep quiet. That's all he's asking. That's all Devil wants."

And what about Luca? He wants to be a tough guy, I'm thinking. Maybe he is. Rolling around with the

Devil of Springfield... only a real Sinner would be that close to the head of the syndicate. Driving him around? Waiting in the car while he meets with shady vice mayors... he's gotta be trusted.

Yet, here he is. Here I am.

And I'm pretty sure he's my babysitter.

My mistake. I took him for the help. A hired chauffeur and nothing else. Whatever role he plays in his gang, I guess watching over loose-lipped witnesses is one of them.

I know one thing: Devil wouldn't have left me alive. For all those rumors that he's lost his edge after his kid was born, I doubt it. He didn't hesitate to off Collins tonight, and I can only imagine what the vice mayor did to sign his death warrant.

Did Devil find out that Johnny Winter had every intention of taking over Springfield in the new year, no matter what it took? That the Snowflakes hadn't given up on expanding their territory at all?

Maybe, but that's the least of my problems. Because of the contract I took on, signed by Winter himself, I was in the wrong place at the wrong time.

But I'm alive because of Luca—and I can use that.

I have to bite the corner of my lip to keep my smile from widening.

Holy shit. This is going to be so much fun!

"Want to play checkers?" I ask.

"Excuse me?"

"Checkers," I repeat. "You know the game. Black

and red pieces. You jump them, then say 'king me'? I love checkers. Or," I add, drawing his attention to the television opposite of the couch, "we can see what's on. I don't know if there's cable up here in the boonies, but if there's a TV, there's gotta be something to watch."

Luca lifts his hand, swiping the back of it over his mouth. "You want to watch TV with me? You're not going to beg me to bring you back home?"

I tilt my head. "I could if you want me to. Do you?"

"Not really."

"That's what I thought. I mean, you obviously went to a lot of trouble to get me here. Chains said you wanted me to stick around so I can't imagine you're going to let me go now. Not when you're sure I'm going to run to the first police station I can find and tell the whole world that the head of the Sinners Syndicate is a merciless murderer."

Can he tell I'm being a smart-ass? I'm not so sure, but to really lay it on thick, I shrug my shoulders. "What would happen then? I'm supposed to stay. So if I try to leave and you try to stop me, I get a bullet in my skull courtesy of the gun in your pants? That it?"

"I'd rather not have to do that."

Somehow, I figured that.

Soft touch. Are they kidding? They kidnapped me and stuck me with a soft touch for a babysitter. If it was me, if I'd chained Luca up in the basement, but he broke free, then scared the shit out of me by throwing open the door? I would've shot first, asked questions later.

Of course, I'm a fucking amazing shot. I'd be asking a dead man those questions so I wouldn't be getting any answers, but still. I would've reacted way differently than Luca did.

He's insistent that I'm staying with him. Luca. A good-looking guy. A secluded mountain hideaway that could easily get snowed-in at any moment.

A pair of cuffs and an empty cot in the basement where no one would hear me scream...

Hmm.

"So... checkers? Yes? No?"

His mouth works, but nothing comes out for a moment. He recovers again, quicker this time, though all he can do is tell me that, "This isn't my cabin. I don't know if they have checkers here."

Pity.

"Okay. No checkers. Got it. Anything to eat? I'm feeling a little peckish."

Luca winces.

I'm thinking that's a 'no' on the food sitch, too.

Glancing down, I pluck at the t-shirt beneath my leather jacket. "What about clothes? You don't want me going anywhere to turn in your boss. Got it. Still, I'd rather not have to wear the same underwear day after day if I don't have to."

"Clothes," he echoes in a strangled voice.

I sigh. "Not too prepared to keep a woman captive, are you?"

Luca swallows roughly. "I can honestly say this was not how I planned on my night going when the boss said he needed a ride."

Huh. I guess not.

Taking a little pity on him, I say, "Size large top. Ten in jeans." I caress the curve of my ass, and Luca's nostrils flare. "Large in panties, too. And if you wanna splurge for a couple of bras, size 36C."

His gaze immediately drops to my chest. I'm not surprised. He's probably looking at my tits and trying to match that to the bra size I gave him. I mean, I practically invited him to gawk at my cleavage.

And maybe I did it on purpose. If I'm stuck here, it'll make the time go that much faster if my captor can be manipulated by sex. Something about the way he's hesitant around me, even though he's supposed to be the one in control, says me that he's at least *attracted*.

I can use that, too.

"If I need anything else," I add, moving near enough to him that I can pat him on the hard chest, "I'll make sure to tell you."

Luca freezes under my touch. I can't tell if that's a good or bad reaction, but I take my hand back, pretending not to notice it all.

"So, your name," he says after a moment, obviously still stuck on that. What is he? A stickler for introductions or something? "Does it start with a H?"

Maybe he is, but he's also so damn *adorable.*

Like he didn't see my 'H' tat in the web of my hand when he was putting those cheap-ass cuffs on me. If he wanted to restrain me, he needed standard-issue police cuffs, not the shit you get for 3.99 at Walmart. Even kinky, furred cuffs would've been better, though my last ex would verify that I could break free of those with enough motivation.

What would he say if I told him I got the tattoo after I dropped a hummingbird crystal figurine at the feet of the first contract I took? That it would be a real noob move to ink the actual bird on my skin, but a tiny 'H'? Who would ever know?

Not Luca.

"Nope." I make another display of looking around. "You work on getting me some clothes. Until then, I'll just have to stick with these. But a shower... I want one of those. Please tell me there's hot running water up here."

"Um. Yeah. Actually, there's a bathroom in the basement. You get your own bed, your own room, and your own bathroom."

I give him an appraising look. "Okay. Maybe you're a little more prepared than I thought. Good. And I hope there's enough hot water otherwise you'll be shivering when you wash up." I pause for a moment. "You are going to be the one staying here with me, right?"

He hesitates for a moment. "Until Devil relieves me or tells me to come home, I'll be here."

Translation: until the Devil of Springfield decides I'm too much trouble and orders his driver to use that Ruger against me.

Nah. That's not going to happen. And if it does...

Well. Playtime will be over for Kylie. Until then—

"You want to join me?" I ask him.

"Join you?" I swear to fucking God, the heights of his cheeks turn *pink*. "You mean, in the shower?"

I shrug. "Sure."

His hand falls behind him, landing on the butt of his gun. "No. I... no. I don't think so."

Me, neither, but it didn't stop me from asking—or seeing what I could get away with so far.

I wink over at Luca. "Worth a shot, ace."

The quick flash of relief on his face switches to a look of confusion. "Ace?"

"Yeah. I don't know. It suits you. You mind?"

He shakes his head, and proving that my read on him is spot-on, he asks, "And what do I call you?"

I laugh, moving toward the open door that leads to the basement. He tightened up when I took my first step, as though he expected me to break for the front entrance, only relaxing when I behaved like the perfect captive by crawling back to my hole.

Though he does frown a little when I tell him: "Nice try, but you still haven't earned it."

Then, pausing on the first step, I curl my fingers around the door so that I can look over my shoulder at

Luca. "Don't forget to lock the door behind me. Wouldn't want your captive to escape."

Then, releasing my hold, I waggle my fingers at Luca, holding my giggle back until I tug the door behind me and start down the stairs.

Only after I hear the tell-tale *snick* that says he took my advice do I let it out.

Yup.

I was right.

This is definitely gonna be *quite* entertaining.

thou shall not...

NINE
CHECKERS

LUCA

Clothes. She needs clothes.

And food.

Shit.

What was I thinking? That I could hide a girl in a basement, lock her away from the world, and my determination to keep her safe would be all that she needs? Fucking idiot. I packed up a couple of changes of clothes before I left my place. Why didn't it occur to me that she'd need some, too?

And if I'm kicking my own ass for being so stupid, it's only because it's easier to focus on that than remember the outright twinkle in her eyes when she invited me to join her in the shower.

It's obvious that was a nervous offer made by someone who doesn't know what to make of the situation they're in. Like it or not, she's at my mercy. I have the gun. I have the orders that I can't let her step foot out of the cabin, or else Devil expects me to use it. And while my boss is one of a handful of people I've told about how I was raised—mainly because our religious trauma was something we had in common and the reason why he allowed me to join the Sinners in the first place—he doesn't know how I struggle with the fifth commandment.

Thou shall not kill.

There are some rules I can't bring myself to break because they've been beaten into me so deeply, it physically aches me to even think of going against them. Taking a life isn't one of them. There might come a day that I'm going to Cross, asking for my ninth tally mark, but I'll hate myself even more if it's because I extinguish her twinkle.

I don't know her name. I don't know anything about her except the initial impression I got of her down on Skid Row, plus how our recent interaction took everything I already believed and spun it on its damn head.

I expected to have to calm her. To soothe her. To make her understand something that most civilians never would. I was prepared for terror. For pleading. For a quick acceptance that, in exchange for her life, she'd keep her silence.

What I didn't expect?

Was for her to break out of the handcuff I put on

her, smash the chain that kept her tethered to the basement cot, and wake me up from the first sleep I had in nearly twenty-four hours by throwing open the door off the side of Burns's living room.

That one was on me. Exhausted yet undeniably amped, like I sucked down one of the energy drinks that Cross seems to live on, I plopped down on the couch after I got her set up downstairs. I planned on keeping her down there as long as it took to get her to understand that she's mine now, at least until Devil can be sure she's no longer a liability. Locking the door was essential, and I could've sworn I did.

At least the basement door, I thought I had. I didn't want to know why Burns had installed an outer lock in the first place—or why his mountain cabin needed a furnished cot supposedly capable of keeping a woman on top of it—but I must've fucked up and not engaged it all the way.

The front door was my mistake. Burns's nearest neighbor is at least three miles away. With the girl safely downstairs, I wasn't worried about someone breaking in. Not only is this a notable cop's hideaway, but with the old snow making it a tough climb as it is, no one would head over here.

No one but me, that is.

I can't let her escape. She's dead if she does, and if I prove myself unreliable to Devil, that's my head, too. She has to stay, and though she seemed to accept that... *Fuck*. It's too easy.

Nothing in my life has been this easy.

What sort of captive *wants* to stay? Oh, sure, she said it's because she doesn't want a bullet in her skull, but instead of swearing she'll do anything to keep herself safe, she asked about food. About clothes.

About *checkers*.

And I have to admit that, watching the slight smirk stretch her gorgeous face, the tease in her husky voice as she called me 'ace' before chiding me for leaving the door unlocked, and the way my cock came to life as soon as she made her mocking offer to join her in her shower... I'm *fucked*.

I already knew I was attracted to her. It only took one glimpse earlier tonight for my breath to catch in my throat. There was something about her. Something I couldn't quite explain, only that it was enough to make me forget my duty for a moment. But that's nothing compared to how I'm currently walking around with an erection pulsing against my suit pants, palming my length as if that'll do anything to get the fucker under control.

Somewhere below my feet, she's naked and wet, enjoying the shower while I do everything I can to resist the urge to do what she offered and join her.

Would I frighten her? If she saw the mark on my arm, would she be afraid—or would she pity me? Would she cover up, or let me see what she looks like naked?

Would she make a move on me to save her skin, or

laugh that I'd ever believe a creature like her would ever pay attention to an awkward, broken man like Luca St. James?

She has no idea just how safe she is with me. I know most of the Sinners. I know their secrets, and I know their vices. Sometimes, it takes the worst kind of men who join a syndicate like ours, not for the fraternity of it, but because they want power. Money.

Pussy.

Not me. All I've ever wanted was freedom, and even if I sold my soul to be Devil's servant, it was better than what I left behind. And I don't just mean Hamilton. I regret what happened there, but those two years are nothing compared to the twenty-two that came before them.

Everyone thinks that the reason I left Hamilton when I was twenty-four was because I lost my cool on a job, three of the crew ended up in jail after a bank job went bust, with one dead even before the others were caught. Leon Martinez took a bullet from an armed security guard, and I took off the second the shots rang out. As the wheelman, I sacrificed the rest of the crew to save my skin.

Part of that is true. A wheelman did lose his nerve, but it wasn't me. That was a new kid called Stache, a last-minute replacement when I had to back out on a long-planned heist.

Kane never came after me because he knew it was Stache's fault the job went belly-up. He even offered me a chance to make up for it—drive for another job he was plotting in Hudson since he was now down *five* members—but I was already in my Mustang, heading out of town, hoping that, this time, it takes longer than two years for my parents to come looking for me again.

Because they did once, and though I'm constantly looking over my shoulder, expecting to see Frank and Val St. James behind me, that's because they're convinced they hold my leash and control their only son even now.

It's been three years since I hunkered down in Springfield. I've avoided them so far—and there are times I honestly begin to think I've broken free of them at last—but then a pretty girl has my blood pumping, my cock responding to her playful overtones, and I'm suddenly back in Oklahoma again.

I'm in the secluded hamlet of Donovan, named after the man who founded and rule the Holy Church of Jesus Devotion, where a population of barely one hundred does what they're commanded to do. And if they don't...

The girl in the basement wasn't the only one in shackles. I removed hers, though, when she asked me to—and it never even occurred to me to refuse—while mine, invisible as they are, are still holding me down nearly twenty-seven years later.

I've always wanted to be free. Now look at me. I'm responsible for being someone else's jailer.

Using the palm of my hand, I shove roughly at my

erection. With everything I have to do now, borrowing the bathroom down the hall to rub one out is a shitty idea. My body needs the release, but I'm an old pro at resisting the temptation.

Don't fall in love, Luca.

Don't let your dick control you.

Don't get your stupid heart broken.

Don't watch the girl you thought you'd spend the rest of your life with accept the prophet's proposal while wearing *your* ring—or be forced to witness it when he fucked her in front of all of us the first time to prove to the entire congregation... the fucking *cult*... that she was a virgin.

Before I lost Emily to Jack Donovan, I never whacked off. Well, no. I got caught once at fourteen by my dad, and when he was done with the belt, I couldn't sit down without pain for a week. He slapped my dick, too, so much that it left a mark, and every time I got an erection in the days that followed, it was agony. Masturbation was a sin. To the HCofJD, everything was a sin, but pleasure without the intent of procreation was unacceptable.

It was a Hell offense. Touch yourself. Hell. Think of touching your girlfriend's boobs. Hell. Sneak your finger into her pussy, though you knew your dick would never get wet until your wedding night. Hell.

I was allowed to kiss her. That was all. A prim kiss on the lips that wasn't enough when the choice came down to the leader of the church and Luca St. James.

I've kissed a handful of women since Emily. God knows I've watched enough porn to try to burn the image of Emily beneath the prophet while every adult member of the church witnessed the act in awe—and dismay—as she became Donovan's bride.

Once I was out of Oklahoma, beating my meat became my first attempt at rebellion. My parents disowned me. They thought I was the devil reborn. A little jerking off and fantasizing over being the one to make Emily mew like that is what you'd expect from a sinner.

It was how I showed my defiance, even if I still can't bring myself to have penetrative sex until I find the woman I'll choose to marry.

Brainwashing goes fucking deep, I tell you. I've spent five years trying to shake it off, even going so far as to visit the girls who work the upstairs of the Playground to finally say I'd done it for once and for all. But I couldn't. It's not even the fear of eternal damnation that had me losing my erection whenever I tried. Melissa even gave me my first blow job to see if that would help me keep it for the main event. It didn't, and I never went back upstairs again.

Waiting until marriage... it's the idea that sex belongs between two people who are in love. Who are bonded in the eyes of the church and the lord. Who belong to each other.

I know better than to believe that shit now as a grown man, so many years removed from the church.

Tell that to my poor cock.

He's listening now, and so am I. The pipes somewhere in the cabin are creaking. My prisoner is in the shower, and instead of my dick deflating at that thought, I nearly cream my pants at the fantasy of that fascinating woman giving me another one of her heart-stopping smirks before slowly dropping to her knees in front of me...

I grit my teeth, shake my head, and double-check that the lock's engaged. Once I have, I finish the tour of the cabin I neglected to do before I passed out on the couch before.

The Burnses' bedroom is off-limits. He gave me permission to borrow their room during my stay, but it didn't seem right to lay down in their marriage bed, especially knowing that they fuck on it. I already have to pretend like a recently married couple—together for about two years or so—wouldn't take a trip up to their cabin and bang right away on the couch since that's where I'll be spending my nights until I have the girl downstairs under my control...

My dick twitches at the thought.

I ignore it since, damn it, we both know that's not what I mean.

She's made it clear that she has integrity. Morals. If given the chance, she's turning Devil in. I can't... I can't let that happen. So I still have to do whatever it takes to get her to side with me.

To fall for me.

To *love* me, even knowing that I'll never be able to do the same for her in return.

My dick twitches again, calling me a fucking liar.

No. *No.* There's a difference between lust and love, and after spending all of my hormonal teen years hoping that Emily would take pity on me and at least let me have a peek at her tits, I know the difference. Twenty-seven years of pent-up sexual frustration has me looking at such a pretty girl and reacting.

Love at first sight exists. I know that, even if I've never experienced that myself. Look at Rolls and Nicolette. The Sinners Syndicate's fixer knew the waitress would be his the moment he met her. He stayed away because he was her boss, and it wouldn't be right when he had all the power... but he didn't stay away forever. Now they're married, and the power imbalance doesn't seem to bother either one of them anymore—

Shit, Luca. There's a difference between the manager of the Playground thirsting after a waitress he hired. But an impulsive driver having impure thoughts about the woman he drugged and kidnapped?

Focus on the job. Prove yourself to Devil.

Save the girl.

That's all I can hope for.

And it begins with a phone call to Officer Mason Burns.

He answers on the third ring. "Burns here."

"Hi. It's, uh, Luca. Luca St. James."

"Oh, right. The driver in my cabin with the— yeah, yeah. How are you?"

Could be better.

My aching dick agrees.

"I'm alright."

"You settled in? Find the place okay?"

That's the least of my worries. "Yup. Thanks."

"Don't mention it. I'm doing this favor for Devil, and I'll make sure he owes me."

Another reason why I have to turn this girl onto our side. Because I asked him to let me keep her, Devil's now in debt to Burns because of the cabin. He might owe the cop, but I owe the boss.

I'll probably owe Burns, too, since he goes on to tell me that I can help myself to anything I find in his place while I'm here. Since that's the reason why I'm calling, I ask him about what I should do if there's something I *can't* find.

"That's easy," he tells me. "Place an order. Either from a local store or online. It'll reach you. I mean, unless the snow hits the mountains again, or it's Christmas, but tip 'em well enough and you can get everything you need delivered to the cabin."

"Oh." I should've realized that. I guess, being sleep-deprived and way too attracted to my captive has my head all fucked up. "Great. That's good to know."

"Anything else you have to ask? Or to tell me? 'Cause I'm on duty, but you can always reach out again if you need something."

My upbringing and hesitation to break the rules that both my parents and myself had set for me doesn't just revolve around sex. That's a huge fucking issue for me, obviously, but it also makes it nearly impossible for me to lie. I just... my stomach gets twisted in knots whenever I try, and my honesty was another perk when Devil hired me on.

Which is why, before I even think about what I'm going to say, I blurt out: "Oh. I should tell you... I'm sorry about the chains."

"Hang on. Hey, Rook. Hold the corner, would you? Let me finish this call." Through the connection, I hear the winter wind whipping past, then Burns's voice again. "Okay. Now, what's that about my chains?"

"Um. Well. The girl I'm watching over for Devil... she kind of broke them."

I don't know what I thought his response would be. I've been around Burns more than a few times, mostly when I drive Devil to meet with the street cop. I can never get a good read on the guy. He seems so charming and good-spirited at times, but I was a disciple of Jack Donovan. I know a twisted soul when I see one, and Burns has a dark side.

Not just enough to sell out the people of Springfield, choosing to work for the syndicate instead, either. There's something else there. Something I can't place.

Which is probably why I'm so taken aback when he starts laughing.

"Well, fuck. I'm gonna have to make it up to my

angel until I can get a replacement. Nothing gets her hotter than when I have her trapped beneath me. She's sweet, but when I get the chains on her... Shame, St. James. You could've had some fun in the basement with my setup. Hey, you still should. You want to make that girl a Sinner? Sin a little with her first."

Fuck.

My cheeks heat up.

Like I said, my religious upbringing screwed me up. I'll be the first to admit it. It did a number on anyone who was unlucky enough to have parents conned by Jack Donovan into worshipping his corrupt, hypocritical ass.

The first time I kissed Emily, she cried because she thought I just sentenced us both to an eternity in Hell. The way she ran to her parents to confess, how she was so damn scared, allowed us the permission to peck without any repercussions.

In the years that followed, during our long, long courtship, we pushed the boundaries of what we thought we could get away with. Both of us talked endlessly about what our wedding night would be like —until Donovan noticed just how beautiful a twenty-one-year-old Emily was and took her for himself.

And she *let* him.

It's been five years. Closer to six now that it's December. I was kicked out of the church when it became obvious that I couldn't even pretend to be happy for the newlyweds. My parents, long sure I was a demon in disguise, made that very clear the night I broke the seventh commandment for the first time.

Thou shall not steal.

Donovan stole my girl.

I stole a key—and then a car.

It was as fair as I could make it...

I shake my head. Too many bad memories drudged up tonight. All my fault, too. That happens when I feel like I'm losing control over my life. Over my body. Over every-damn-thing.

Sleep, I tell myself. I need some more sleep.

But first, I have shit to do. So, after quickly ending the call with the cop, I start looking up local stores that will deliver to the cabin. I need clothes. To fill the kitchen and the pantry up. To provide anything my captive is going to require while I have her here. The clothes are easy. So is the food, and the necessities like pads, a toothbrush, toilet paper, and deodorant.

Now, where can I find someone to bring me a game of checkers?

thou shall not...

TEN
BORED

KYLIE

Not gonna lie, I was kind of hoping my pretty boy captor would take me up on my invitation and join me downstairs.

His reaction wasn't like anything expected. I mean, he's a mafia guy. Low man on the pole as the dude driving the leader around, sure, but he has a gun. A snub-nosed Ruger. He's armed—and I'd bet my latest commission fee that he's never pulled that trigger in a life-or-death situation before.

Is he a good criminal? Talk about an oxymoron. He stole me, but there's no denying the flash of shame that crossed his face when he realized that he's way underprepared to *keep* me. Even a regular woman would need more than he has, but Luca had the misfortune to nab a high-maintenance, exacting chick like me.

He wants a mountain prisoner? I'm game. It seems like it's going to be fun. Granted, my outlook on life is a lot different from that of an ordinary person. If he annoys me, I've got my strychnine and, like, ten other ways to end him before I take his keys, steal whatever car he used to transport me here and head back to the city.

And why should I? After what happened last night, I think I'm owed a little Christmas vacation. I was planning on finishing my contract and then flitting around, spending the holidays by myself before heading to Florida to visit my parents, Lindy, and Charlie. A mountain cabin getaway with a guy as easy on the eyes as this Luca?

I like the idea of it more than I should.

I'm a healthy twenty-six-year-old with a pretty high libido. He's gotta be close to my age, and unlike Devil, he doesn't wear a ring on his finger. Sure, that doesn't mean he doesn't have a lady—or a guy—back in Springfield. It's possible. Consider his looks, more than likely. But what if he got the babysitting gig because he's like me: no real ties to anyone but the life we've chosen?

I'll run with that. After all, if I'm stuck here, seducing Luca and using him to pass the time sounds like a plan.

I'm Kylie Ferguson. I *always* have a plan.

Sometimes, I don't think them through. I'll admit that. I definitely caught him off-guard by breaking out of the cuffs and the chains so easily, then making no move to leave the cabin. Now, do I believe he'd actually shoot me if I scoffed and tried to leave? My initial impression is a seventy/thirty split. He has a job to do, and if Devil gave it to him, he'll do it.

But luckily for Luca, I don't want to leave. Why should I? He has to take care of me for as long as I continue to act like I give a shit that Devil killed Springfield's vice mayor. Please. I was on Skid Row to commit murder myself. Who am I to judge? But he obviously thinks I'm some poor innocent woman who saw too much.

I can use that.

So far, captivity isn't half bad. As long as he doesn't insist that I sit in a dark, gloomy basement in chains, I'll be okay. Like he said, there's a pretty decent bath-room downstairs, with a toilet and a shower stall and —*yes*—hot running water. The cot isn't as plush as the one in my room at my parents' condo, but when you spend your life in hotels, motels, and hostels, you get used to hard-ass mattresses. I'll survive.

I don't have my phone, but that could be a good thing. I've been meaning to unplug for a minute and usually do when I'm not looking to take on a job for a few days. Not having a TV is going to be a deal-breaker if Luca doesn't decide to be my entertain-ment, but I saw one upstairs. Once I can get him to understand that I'll be the most willing captive in his kidnapping career, maybe he'll let me upstairs to watch it. Or, if he's going to keep me locked down here, I can bat my lashes and get him to bring it down.

Though, to be honest, I would rather he take one for the team and let me have some fun with him. That's basically the outline of my plan. Be the model captive. Don't try to escape, only ask for what I need, and do what Kylie does best: keep him off-guard. After our exchange upstairs, I'm not worried he'll hurt me. He's my babysitter, right? He wants me to side with him and his boss.

I might as well let him think that's a possibility.

Until then, I'll do what I can to get close to him. Have a little fun if he's down for that. Without my phone, I can't get in contact with my client anyway. As it is, Winter's probably waiting for me to confirm that I made my kill. Then again, since I'm not off the grid— and he clearly has other eyes on the city while he's tending to his enterprise elsewhere—he's gotta know. And that's assuming the news of the vice mayor's murder doesn't get out on its own. I mean, the guy was pretty high-profile in Springfield. I wouldn't be surprised if the people there start wondering who did it.

Since Devil's obviously not claiming the hit, why shouldn't the Hummingbird?

Too bad I didn't think to drop my figurine on Skid Row before Luca manhandled me into the trunk. I had to hide that and my knife under the interior instead, but it would've been so much if I left my calling card behind in Springfield.

Who knows? I might even suggest the idea to Luca once I have the driver wrapped around my little finger. He doesn't need to know I'm the Hummingbird; in fact, I'm going to do everything I can to prevent him from learning my little secret. But over the years, my rep's taken on a life of its own. He has to have heard of me.

Why not give me credit for the kill?

Until then, I'll play the role of the damsel in distress, Kylie-style. And when I'm not having fun anymore, I'll get my revenge for him daring to drug me, then I'll figure out my next move.

He has a gun. I'm banking on the fact that he has a phone, too, plus a car.

And, most importantly, no idea who he's dealing with.

I SHOULDN'T HAVE FLIPPANTLY REMINDED HIM TO LOCK the basement door behind me.

It's been hours since I came down here. Part of me hoped he'd follow after me when I mentioned taking a shower, but he obviously didn't. I even left the bathroom door open so he knows I'm not hiding down here, but by the time I finished, grabbing one of the towels hanging off the hook in the small room, there was no sign of my captor.

That didn't change.

I'm hungry. I found a box of slightly outdated granola bars in the fridge for some reason, plus three bottles of chilled water. I drank one, choked down a bar, and waited for him to check on me. When he didn't, I checked the door. Locked. I didn't want to push my luck and kick it open with my boot, so I banged a couple of times.

No answer.

That's about the time I started to think my impression of Luca was waaaay off. Did he decide to leave me down here to rot?

Um. No.

No. He did not.

One downside of being in a windowless basement with no phone? I have no idea what time it is. It's been long enough that I'm boooored. Hungry and bored, and leaning back against the headboard, staring up at the ceiling, my heart jumps when I hear the gentle knock coming from the door upstairs.

I'm being held captive. He's the guy watching over me.

And he just knocked.

Biting back an amused smile at just how easy this is going to be, I call out, "I'm decent, if that's what you're thinking."

Considering I hear the door ease open, plus the light steps of his sneakers as he comes down the stairs, it probably was.

Now, I didn't lie. Not really. I *am* decent.

I'm also just wearing only the skimpy towel I found in the bathroom.

All the important bits are covered so I don't know why he comes to a short stop at the bottom of the stairs, eyes locked on me.

To be fair, part of me was looking for a reaction from Luca. Part of me just didn't want to put my dirty clothes back on. I twisted my hair up in a bun while I was washing off. When I didn't see a hairbrush or any curly girl hair products in the bathroom, I decided to leave my mop like it was for now until I have the supplies to do a deep wash.

Something else to add to the list of things I'm gonna need...

And if those boxes and bags piled up in his arms are any clue, all I have to do is ask for it and my captor will find a way to get it for me.

Clothes. He brought me clothes, and in the right size, too. Nothing fancy. Plain jeans, a couple of t-shirts, a bra, and a six-pack of basic underwear. All online buys, and items he would've picked out with same-day delivery.

His tongue darting out, dabbing his bottom lip a little nervously, he adds that he's also expecting a grocery delivery.

The whole time he's talking, he keeps going from looking at my face, his eyes dropping to my naked legs on display before he catches on that he's ogling me and quickly looks away.

I have my answer, then. Whether or not he has a partner back home, there's definitely a spark flying between us. I sense the chemistry like electric shocks floating through the air, and I don't think I'm the only one.

So I do what I always do: I flirt, also Kylie-style.

"Well, gee. You sure know how to make your prisoners feel welcome. I was beginning to think we were both in over our heads, but maybe not. So, what is it? This your thing? Kidnapping helpless victims and keeping them in your basement?"

I surprised him. I still think he's waiting for me to break down in tears or something, and the tease in my voice has thrown him for a loop.

He rubs the back of his hand over his mouth before admitting, "It's not mine."

"What? Your thing? Or your basement?"

"The basement. It belongs to... a friend of mine."

I glance over my shoulder, eying the handcuffs hanging off the headboard. "Makes it weirder, you know. Just saying."

He clears his throat. "Besides. You're the only girl I've ever had to take."

"And that makes me get the fuzzies," I tease, sticking the tip of my tongue out through the gap between my teeth. "Knowing I'm the first chick you ran off with."

A muscle flexes in his jaw. "It's not like that."

"Mm."

I'm fucking with him. It's just too, too easy. Besides, as grateful as I am that he cared enough to get me food and clothes, he still *stole* me. I'm not going to let him forget that.

"Anyway," he adds, "it's not that weird. My friend comes out to the cabin with his wife when they want to get away from the city. He's not taking prisoners, either."

I peek at the handcuffs again. "Those are theirs? The chains, too?" At Luca's nod, I admit, "Okay. That makes a lot more sense why they'd be down here. If there's one thing I can say about me, it's that I don't yuck another couple's yum."

"Couple?" he echoes. His Adam's apple bobs. "You, uh... you involved with someone?" His striking green eyes flicker to my hand. "Is that the 'H'?"

Wouldn't he like to know?

I offer him a sly smile. "What's the matter, Luca? Didn't you do your research before you took me? Or after?"

"How? I don't even know your name."

He did something nice for me. Sure, it's the least he can do after he tossed me in a trunk and chained me up down here, but I'm in a much better mood now that I know how easy it's going to be to manipulate this guy.

I decide to play the game with him just a little.

Shaking my pointer finger, I tell him, "Uh uh. I see

what you're doing. You ask me if I'm seeing someone. Not because you give a shit, but because you're trying to figure out if someone's gonna come looking for me."

"What? No, I—"

See? Easy.

"Okay. You don't have to torture me or anything for the info, ace. I'll tell you."

"Torture? Who said anything about torture?"

I give him a look that says *he* did. "My parents live in Florida. I have a sister. She's married. Second time around, and we're all hoping this one will work out. Me? I've never been married. Haven't had a serious relationship since college." All true. The thing about being whoever the clients expect you to be? As amusing as that is, sometimes I just want to be myself. Why not now? "I went to Rutgers. That's in New Jersey. Got a BA in history, but not my MRS. I'm only twenty-six, though, so, like, what's the rush? My job takes me everywhere so I don't have a boss looking for me, either. I'm the best chick you could've picked to steal. So how's that? Satisfied?"

His forehead wrinkles. "You'll tell me all that, but not your name?"

That's right, buddy. Keep up.

"I did say you need to earn it." I jerk my chin at him. "So why don't you tell me something about yourself so I don't just keep thinking of you as my creepy captor."

The 'creepy' was a nice touch. I know from the way

he winces that he'll tell me just as much as I did—and, like me, it'll be all true.

"Okay. We're going to be spending the time together, so it's only fair. My name's Luca. Luca St. James. I'm twenty-seven. I don't have any family. Not anymore," he says, and that sparks my interest. Are they dead? No contact? Interesting, especially when he adds, "Not unless you count the Sinners."

Luca has been standing this whole time, on his feet next to the cot once he laid out all of the clothes near mine. For the first town, he lowers himself so that we're on the same level. "If I can't get you to prove to Devil that you'll keep quiet, he'll kill you, and I'll feel bad about that. Oh, and I'm single, too."

Completely disregarding the part about how his boss wants me dead, I grin over at him. "Hitting on me, ace?"

He hurries to his feet. "What? No."

"Pity." And I mean it. "Well, now that we've gotten our introductions out of the way, I'd like to get dressed. Close your eyes if you want. I don't care. But I am dropping the towel."

I give him a moment to turn around or close his eyes. When he doesn't—whether because he thinks I'm bluffing, or he hopes I'm not—I swallow my smile. Oh, yeah. He's definitely attracted to me.

Good.

I drop the towel, reaching for a pair of panties.

Lifting my ass up off the cot, Luca swallows roughly as my bare tits bounce with the motion as I shimmy the panties into place.

"Well?" His voice is strangled, and it really is a shame that his gaze seems pinned to a point over my head now. "Do they fit?"

"Perfectly," I purr. Then, taking pity on the guy, I snag a shit and pull it on over my head so that I'm just as covered as I was before. "So... how does this work?" I ask. "I just stay down here for now?"

His eyes meet mine. "Until I believe you when you say you won't escape."

"I won't."

And... Luca doesn't believe me. "Fine. Then tell me what you saw last night."

I could say nothing. That's what he wants to hear. That I'll go along with what his boss wants and pretend I was momentarily struck dumb and blind.

But then this would be over before I had any real fun with Luca, and after the way he just looked at me? That would be a *shame* shame.

So, with the most innocent expression I can muster, I tell him, "I saw a man coming around the corner after three shots rang out. Your boss. The Devil of Springfield. He mentioned a corpse so he must've killed a guy."

Luca shakes his head. "I'll come back later with dinner. Just... just behave, okay?"

I'll try.

And, okay, that's a lie because he doesn't even make it halfway up the stairs before I call out again with a grin, "Don't forget to lock the door, ace."

thou shall not...

ELEVEN
KYLIE

LUCA

I don't know how I made it upstairs with the lead pipe in my pants.

Ever since I accepted that I would be stuck in close quarters with the most tempting woman I've ever seen in my whole fucking life, I've warned my cock to behave. I'm no rapist. There's no way she can consent under these conditions. If anything, she's using the one advantage she has: her body, and my obvious attraction to it.

To *her*.

Fuck me. I shouldn't have looked. When she dared me by telling me she was about to drop her towel, I should have taken her at her word and realized that she—*she,* because in spite of everything she told me...

that I want to believe is true... I still don't know her name—would do it. That she wasn't bluffing.

Because she wasn't.

I've seen tits. Touched them, too. Just because I've never stuck my dick inside of a welcoming pussy, that doesn't mean I've cut myself off from women. Not completely, at least. Considering the amount of porn I watch when I'm off duty, I've seen all types of tits. Real ones. Fake ones. Perky ones. Saggy ones.

Hers are fucking *perfect*.

I looked longer than I should have. They're the right size for me, each one looking like they would nestle securely against my palms. Her nipples are a dusky brown color, hard and poking out due to the chill in the basement. My mouth watered to taste them, and I forced myself to swallow roughly before she noticed how I was panting like a damn dog.

Is she messing with me? Definitely. I'm starting to get an idea of what to expect from my too-willing captive. It's like she *wants* to stay. I can't deny that she's obviously hitting on me now, though if it's to save her skin, I get it. When I'm the only one keeping her safe from the boss, it's no wonder that I'll start to look pretty good. She might even be biding her time, hoping that I'll form a bond with her, making it easy for me to lower my guard and help her escape.

But if that's the case... why does she keep reminding me to lock her down? Because she wants me to stay away, or because she's trying to see if I *will*?

I don't know. I don't know anything—

—except she's single, and I kind of wish I didn't know *that*. Not when I'm already more drawn to her than I have any right to be.

That's why, instead of running to the bathroom and giving in to that attraction, I pointedly ignore it as I pull my phone out of my pocket.

The service up here is better than I thought it would be. That I don't have any missed calls or messages since the last time I checked isn't a surprise. I'm a quiet guy. I keep to myself. Unlike some of the other Sinners, I don't go to the Playground to party or to show off my devil tat. I'm either driving the Devil of Springfield around, or I'm working on my Ford Mustang rebuild. All of my calls involve Sinners biz.

Devil knows I'm up here. He won't be messaging me his location anytime soon, and though he promised to check in and see how it's going, he's a very busy man with a family he worships. If I hear from him by the end of the weekend, that'll be more like the boss.

I won't just reach out to him, either. Even though I have more access to the boss than the other Sinners on my level, I know better than to just call him up and bother him.

But there is someone I *can* call.

With Genevieve practicing for her upcoming performances, Cross will be more available than usual. At this hour, he's probably sitting in his tattoo shop unless Devil needs him. Hoping that he's free and not in the middle of holding his needle, I call him.

He answers almost right away.

"Luca, hey. I was wondering if I'd hear from you. I talked to Devil earlier. He said I might. How did the meet with the vice mayor go? Rolls was unusually tight-lipped when I asked him."

That's because Rolls is Devil's right-hand man. Though Rolls and Cross are old high school friends, if Devil says 'keep quiet', Rolls shuts his mouth.

I know why, too. Cross is an easygoing, chill guy most of the time. He has a few triggers. CSA is one. So is fire. Lately, though, it's Genevieve Libellula—and his hatred for Johnny Winter and his crew.

He's been obsessively searching for some sign of the Snowflakes. If only to protect his butterfly, he wants to go after Winter himself. Devil disagrees. He wants to make a statement by taking down the Snowflakes. Damien Libellula, too. Cross knew he couldn't come to Blockbuster last night to confront the vice mayor himself, but he's probably been dying for an update.

I wish I had better news for him. "If it's not out now, it will be soon. Devil had to off Collins after he admitted he was on Winter's payroll. He didn't really have more than that." Then, because I know he'll ask, I add, "No lead on where Winter is hiding out, either. They did everything online. Tanner's probably combing through Collins's accounts right now so maybe there will be something out of that."

Cross mutters a curse under his breath. "Yeah. I figured as much. Word on the street is that Collins bit it, but that it wasn't a Sinner who pulled the trigger."

Really? "Then who?"

"The Hummingbird."

Wait... didn't he mention something about a person with that name at his studio last night? Not like the little figurine he was playing with *hummingbird*, but someone who had a 'the' before it?

"Who's the Hummingbird?"

"You haven't heard about him?" Cross sounds surprised. "I thought I told you."

He started to, then somehow we changed the subject. "Nah. I don't think so."

"Shit, Luca. The Hummingbird is an assassin. A hired hitman. This... this contract killer who burned down my studio because Mickey Kelly paid him to. That's why I found the hummingbird. It's his... I don't know... symbol or some shit. He leaves it behind so everyone knows he pulled the job. There wasn't one this time, but he's been busy enough lately that people are starting to talk."

And I'm only just hearing about it when I'm so far away from the city?

"We've got a killer in Springfield targeting Sinners?" I ask, stunned.

"That's the worst part. It's not just Springfield. This

guy is a savage, dropping people all over the country in messy ways. Like gluing the window shut and lighting a fire so I burn to death *messy*."

We all wondered if that was on purpose. In our circle, everyone knows Cross has trauma, even if—like me—he keeps it to himself. His family died in a fire. For him to nearly go out the same way, that's fucked up. Up until now, he thought Mickey did it for payback after Cross went for his cock. But to hear that he hired a guy to do it, and that the guy makes a habit of shit like that?

"So... what? They think this Hummingbird dick killed Collins? He's a bastard for what he did to you, but maybe that's a good thing. It won't fall back on us."

It won't fall back on Devil.

And if no one thinks Devil did it, and some fresh-faced twenty-six-year-old stunner tells the cops that it *was* Devil, not only does the Hummingbird get away with trying to kill Cross, but he might be pissed off that people were blaming him for a hit he didn't do...

Shit. That means I still have to go through with this.

"Maybe. But I'm not worried about some faceless killer coming after me again. It's been months, and Damien gave us the best security system money could buy for our new place. Let him try to break in and set a fire. I'll be ready for him."

Thou shall not kill—unless you're saving your fiancée... and getting vengeance.

I MAY NOT BE THE WORLD'S BEST COOK, BUT I'VE learned how to fend for myself since living on my own. In the beginning, it was a lot of take-out, frozen chicken nuggets, and peanut butter and jelly sandwiches, all 'garbage' food that the prophet wouldn't let us have in Donovan. And while I gorged myself on all the snacks I had been deprived of, the tiny apartment I lived in had a stove. Before long, I was making simple meals.

I'm not sure what I'm supposed to feed the girl in the basement. Figuring that pasta with butter or sauce is a safe bet—unless she's gluten-sensitive, then I'm fucked—I put on a pot of water to boil.

While that's working, I finish putting away the groceries I ordered. I know I'll need more. I've barely filled the fridge with what I got, and the cabinets in the kitchen have plenty of space for things like canned goods, boxes of cereal, and other non-perishables.

I'm just glad they showed up after all. I was beginning to think I screwed up when I made the order, but toward the end of my conversation with Cross, I heard a doorbell. I rushed him off the phone, only giving the screen a puzzled look when he tells me to enjoy my Christmas vacation—before realizing that that must be how Devil's explaining away my disappearance for now—then answered the door.

My groceries were there, being dropped off by a

blank-faced kid of about nineteen who nodded when I handed him an extra twenty as a tip for coming out in the cold. It started to flurry a little, too, with a dusting of snow covering a package that must've been dropped off earlier without me knowing.

The pasta is done and ready in less than twenty minutes. Only after I finish cooking it do I realize that Burns's cabin doesn't have a strainer. I do my best not to spill the long spaghetti strands as I dump the pot of starchy water into the sink. A tablespoon of butter to keep them from sticking, then a quick stir before I figure that's as good as it's going to get.

The pot goes on the kitchen table. I pop open the jar of sauce and place it next to the pot. I keep the stick of butter out, and two of the plastic forks I ordered since giving her access to a metal one just doesn't seem like a great idea when I'm still getting a read on the girl.

Do I think she's going to stab me with a fork? Of course not. But, well, you never know.

I grab the other package that came earlier and put it on the other side of the table so she can't miss it. All that taken care of, I run my fingers through my hair nervously before going to the basement door and knocking.

I listen, a smile tugging on my lips as I hear her voice lift up and say, "Still decent, ace. And I mean it this time."

My cock twitches.

Fuck. As if I needed a reminder of how she was wearing nothing but a tiny ass towel when I went down earlier. I nearly swallowed my whole damn tongue when I saw her stretched out on the cot like that, and a pang of remorse hits me when I realize that she's probably fully dressed in one of the few outfits I ordered her.

I take a moment to adjust my semi, trying to wrest back a sliver of control. When that proves to be useless, I untuck my t-shirt, hoping that'll hide the bulge that will inevitably be pushing against my jeans again anytime I'm around her.

I go down. Like I thought, she's changed into the peachy-colored t-shirt and one of the tight black leggings I picked out because, fuck, I'm a glutton for punishment. Even from this angle on the stairs, I can see how the clingy fabric molds itself around the side of her ass.

If she bends over in front of me, I'll *explode.*

Swallowing the lust rising up in my throat, I force myself to look at the wall behind her. "Just wanted to let you know that the groceries came. I made dinner. It's ready."

"Where is it?"

Oh. Right. She's supposed to be my captive. Why wouldn't she figure that I'd plate it up and bring it down so she can eat in the basement?

Why? Because I wanted to sit next to her at the table and eat *with* her.

"It's upstairs. There's a table in the kitchen… and since you said you won't escape… I thought we could eat together. But if you'd rather I get your plate and bring it down—"

"And give up on the chance to go upstairs again? Please. I'm coming." With more enthusiasm than I expect, she bounces off of the cot. "So, what are we having? I'm starving."

A pang of guilt twists my stomach in knots. Of course she is. It's already evening the day after I tossed her in the trunk. I didn't have anything to offer her earlier so unless she found something down here, she's gone all day without a meal.

"Sorry about that. But I made spaghetti. There's butter and sauce if you want it, and a box of cookies for dessert if you're still hungry."

Her face brightens. "I fucking love spaghetti! Red sauce? Tell me it's red sauce."

"It's the traditional kind. At least, that's what the jar says."

"That's my favorite!" Look at that. Mine, too. "What about the cookies? I'm a sugar fiend, so I won't turn down any of them, but if they're chocolate chip, I'll love you forever."

"It's a mixed box," I admit, "but I think it said it had a couple."

"Dibs on the chocolate chip."

She can have all of them if it'll make her smile like

that. "I've got something else for you, too," I tell her, following her up the stairs.

She tosses me a look over her shoulder. "Be careful, ace. Keep spoiling me like that and you might have a harder time getting rid of me than you'd ever guess."

Is that a promise?

With an impish shrug of her shoulder, she dances up the stairs. For a heartbeat, I watch her ass jiggle, and before I know it, she's gone—and I'm still standing stunned on the stairs.

Shit.

I jog after her. Hoping like hell she didn't take my momentarily distraction to flee after all, I look around the empty living room, then head for the kitchen when I hear the tinkling sound of her amused laughter.

She's holding the box I ordered earlier in her hands. It came with only an address sticker on it—that I peeled off, just in case—but she can see what it is from the name and picture splashed across the lid.

Her smile could make a man do a lot of fucking terrible things, but I'm quickly becoming one of them because it nearly brings me to my knees. "You got me checkers?"

I did, and I've never been happier to spend 12.99.

I shrug. "You asked for it."

Her gaze drops to the box, her smile widening. Then, setting the box of checkers back down on the kitchen table, she reaches for the pot of spaghetti.

So... did she like it? Is that why she was smiling? Or was that because she just wanted dinner? Maybe—

"Kylie."

My thoughts running a mile a minute, I miss what she said. "What's that?"

"My name. It's Kylie." She grabs the serving spoon and starts dishing out some spaghetti onto her plate. "You earned it, ace."

I watch approvingly as she piles it up, then douses the noodles in sauce. As soon as she plops down in one of the two seats, pulling the plate toward her, I ask, "Do I get to be 'Luca' then?"

She glances up at me, spaghetti twirled expertly around her fork. "Would you prefer it?"

I think about it for a second.

"I like being your 'ace', Kylie."

And I like the taste of her name on my tongue, too.

It's even better than spaghetti.

thou shall not...

TWELVE
CUCUMBER

KYLIE

Who ever thought getting my ass kicked at checkers would be a turn-on?

Then again, there's something about this guy. I don't know what it is. I mean, I like him. He's like nothing I ever expected from a guy affiliated with one of the local gangs who run Springfield. He's not a fuckboi, either. He just seems so... good.

He cooks me three meals a day. A simple breakfast, a basic lunch, and a hot dinner which, I have to say, is way more than my last, like, four boyfriends did for me. It doesn't have to be fancy. It has to be filling, and he gets bonus points for even doing all the dishes afterward.

I'll give Luca credit. He really took my teasing to heart. When I taunted him for being unprepared to

153

keep someone a captive up here... he's done a complete one-eighty in the last week.

It doesn't stop with three meals a day, either. There's no laundry facilities here. When I ran out of clean clothes, he had another order for me delivered the same day. And it's not like he's rich. During our endless checkers games, I poke and prod and try to get as much information out of him as I can so I know that much.

I tell myself that, deep down, I'm still the Hummingbird. If I ever have to take out Luca, the more I know about him, the easier it will be. And after a week in the cabin, even I can't pretend that I'm basically interrogating him for any other reason than that I'm curious.

Sometimes, he humors me. Sometimes, he sighs, then answers my questions as best he can without giving away Sinners' business.

And then, sometimes, he turns the questions around on me. Which would be fine if he didn't eventually end most of our conversations by whooping my butt at checkers *and* pleading with me to throw my lot in with his boss.

At this point, I should just throw him a bone. I kind of started to feel a little bad about how worried he is about me. He really believes that, if I can't be swayed, I'll end up dead. Not likely, especially since I never would've gone to the cops with what I saw, but he's so... so *earnest*.

But I'm not an idiot. If I finally shrug and agree, he'll be relieved—but if his boss isn't just stringing him along, telling him what he wants to hear before he finally takes matters into his own hands, then that's it. He won't have any reason to be my babysitter anymore.

I can already sense that we've been here too long. His boss probably needs him, his buddy probably wants his cabin back, and he's gotta be tired of buying everything I require. I even tried to give him the couple of dollars I had in my jacket pocket. Luca refused.

I'm his responsibility, after all.

Of course, then I retaliated by asking for a couple of things that I *could* use. I mean, if he really thinks he has to take care of me—and it's obvious he's not about to give me the one thing I'm dying for at the moment—why not take him up on that offer?

We're at an impasse now. He's becoming more and more determined to get me to agree with him. I don't want to go home anytime soon since I kind of like being his captive so I impishly refuse.

Because of that, we've learned which topics of conversation to dance around, and what questions are safe to ask. I've discovered that Luca's favorite movie is an 80s classic, *Die Hard,* that he didn't see for the first time until he was an adult. He's an only child; and that's all I've gotten out of him about his family. He likes the color blue. He's a Gemini... and that's about it.

I still don't know why he wears that key on a chain around his neck.

I don't know why, even when the fire in the fire-place cranks up the heat upstairs, he keeps his long sleeves covering his arms all the way to his wrists.

And I don't know what he's doing as a Sinner...

That one bothers me the most, and after the fourth straight game of checkers where I didn't even come close—and I'm beginning to regret even bringing up this particular game in the first place—I finally blurt out the question that's been haunting me for days.

"Okay. I gotta know. How did a nice guy like you get mixed up with all this mafia bullshit?"

Luca was resetting the game board. He's the black pieces, I'm the red, and since I hate the tediousness of putting the pieces on the board, I let him do it.

He pauses. "Do you really want to know?"

Desperately.

I give him a nonchalant shrug of one of my shoulders. "Well, yeah. It's just... like I said, you seem so nice. A good guy. You've been great to me. Five stars, you know? But then I remember that you're part of the Sinners Syndicate. It doesn't make sense. You're not a killer or a dealer or any of that, are you?"

He shakes his head, letting the piece in his hand fall to the tabletop. "I thought you knew. I'm the driver."

"Well, yeah. I saw you in Devil's car. I figured that was your job. But how does that happen? Become a mafia leader's private chauffeur? I can't imagine he hires out for that."

Luca's lips quirk in a crooked smile. "Nah. You're right. I guess you could say I went to him and asked for the job. He didn't really want a driver, but I was pretty motivated." His eyes gleam at me. "And experienced, too."

"You've driven around other murderers?"

Besides me?

"Not like you're thinking." He taps his fingertip against the tabletop. "I was a wheelman."

A wheelman?

Oh.

"You robbed a bank— no. Not you. Some other guys did and you were the one who drove the getaway car? That it?"

I can't keep myself from sounding impressed, and he can tell.

"'Thou shall not steal.' That was the first commandment I ever broke on purpose." He pauses, reaching up, ruffling the top of his hair. "I break that one a lot."

Right. Like he stole *me.*

Wait...

Commandment?

I start to ask him why he would bring up the Ten Commandments—especially since that's a key on his chain, not a cross, so I didn't take him as uber religious or anything—but I stop when I notice that he's rubbing his forearm through his shirt sleeve.

That's not the first time I've picked up on the

nervous gesture, though it is the first time I call him out on it.

"What are you hiding under there?" I ask. "Is that your devil tat? I wanna see it."

Luca drops his hand down to his thigh. "It's not my devil. I have my horns and tail on my bicep."

All Sinners have a tattoo that mark them as members of the syndicate. It's a Springfield thing. Devil insists his guys get a pair of devil horns and a forked tail as a symbol of loyalty to him and the rest of the syndicate. Meanwhile, the Libellula Family all get inked with varying dragonfly designs to mark their affiliation.

I knew Luca would have to have a devil tat somewhere. Maybe it is on his bicep, but he's still hiding something under his sleeve.

And I want to know what it is.

I start to reach for it. If he doesn't want to tell me, I'll look for myself. He can stop me. If he does, I won't push this. But if he lets me...

He doesn't let me.

Luca jumps up from his seat, dashing over to the refrigerator. "Oh. I almost forgot. Look what got delivered today." He reaches in, pulling out something long and slender and green.

I nearly choke on my laugh. "My cucumber!"

I've been asking him for, like, three days now for one. And while I know it's December, and an unusually snowy one at that so it's not like they're in season, I really, really wanted one—and now it's here.

I swallow my giggle. Yes!

He seems pleased by my happy reaction. "The delivery guy only brought one, even though I tried to order a couple. You wanted it so badly, I figured it's one of your favorite things to snack on."

Snack on?

Oh, Luca, no.

"You sweet summer child," I tease, walking over to the sink so that I can wash the cucumber. "I'm not gonna *eat* this."

"You're not?"

"Nope."

The extra pop on the 'p' is so much fun!

His forehead furrows. "If you're not going to eat it, what are you going to do with it?"

I stroke the outside of the cucumber with a paper towel, drying off the peel, then toss the used towel before grinning over at him.

"I'm going to fuck it," I say, rapping the good-sized cucumber against my palm. "Unless you'd rather take its place."

I don't know what shocks him more: how open I am about my intent to masturbate with the cucumber, or that I once again propositioned him to join me downstairs.

Turns out, it's most likely the second one because he suddenly blurts out nervously: "I can't."

I look at the cucumber. I pointedly look at his junk. I can't see what he's packing, but I'm not a size queen. I can take this cuke. Whether he's big or small, thick or as narrow as a carrot, I don't care. It's the motion of the ocean, right? So long as he knows how to use what he has, I'm down.

"I'm sure you can."

He shakes his head. "No. You don't understand."

I don't think I do. "Is it me? You just don't want to fuck me? If it's because I'm your captive, don't worry about it. I'm not doing this because I'm stuck here. Well, no. I *am* doing that because I'm stuck here and I'm bored. Sorry if that hurts your ego... I still think you're pretty hot, Luca... but I find the best way to fight boredom is a couple of orgasms. So, unless it's just me..."

He licks his bottom lip. "It's not you. I mean, you're gorgeous—"

"Thank you."

"And you didn't offend me. I figured you were only offering because no one else is here."

True.

"But I can't."

I should drop it. And maybe it's because I'm taking this as a blow to *my* ego, but I have to ask one more time: "So why not?"

"Because I don't do that. It's... I'm saving myself for marriage," he mumbles.

He's *what*?

I'm confused. I shouldn't be. Sex is a personal choice, and if he wants to have it or not—if he wants to have it with *me* or not—I can respect that. Some people are ready at fifteen. I was seventeen the first time. I know others who waited until they were in college, or freshly graduated.

Some of my old friends just weren't interested. Others have high body counts, and you know what? Good for them. I never did keep, like, a log or anything, but I'm up there. I have casual sex. I have meaningful sex. One-night stands. Even quickies in a dingy bar bathroom so long as the guy has a condom. I'm very open with my sexuality.

Obviously.

But I've known a handful of guys and girls who decided to wait. And, for the most part, it was for the same reason.

Commandments, I think. He mentioned the Ten Commandments.

Oh, boy.

"Is this a religion thing? I mean, I'm not knocking you or anything. You do you, even if that means you're not doing anyone else. I just... wow. That's another shame, ace. We could've had a lot of fun together."

"I know. But it was how I was raised. Now, I'm used to it."

The way he's fisting his hand tells me otherwise.

Hm. We could've had a lot of fun together—and maybe I still can.

"Is it a sin to watch?"

"What?"

"You heard me. I don't know what your religion is."

He gulps. "It's a small church in Oklahoma. The HCofJD." At my blank look, he says, "The Holy Church of Ja— of Jesus Devotion. It's a Christian sect that—"

And I stopped listening.

Hey. If it's a sin, he can look away. But me?

I'm agnostic, and if I want to fuck myself with a cucumber, no bearded man in the sky is going to harsh my vibe.

"But is it a sin for you, Luca? I mean... if I did this and you watched?" Lifting the cucumber to my mouth, I tongue the tip, licking the slightly bumpy exterior. "Or what about this?"

He's not saying a damn word. Lips slightly parted, eyes glazed over with lust, he just stands there as I grip the back of my leggings, plus my panties, and shimmy them down until they're at my knees.

I have just enough give in the fabric to widen my legs and dip the cucumber between them. I squeal when the chill of the cucumber bumps into my clit.

Luca groans, but he's still watching.

"No," he rasps out after a moment. "I don't think it would be a sin if you did that to yourself and I happened to see it."

I angle the cuke, gathering all the juices slicking my pussy so that I can notch it at my entrance.

"What. About. This?"

His eyelids flutter closed. "Fuck me, Kylie..."

I take the cucumber back. "Sorry, ace. That's not allowed. We're not married."

His eyes snap open. "But—"

Nope. No 'buts'.

"Good night, Luca. I hope you enjoy yours." I waggle the cucumber. It's not exactly what I wanted, but waste not, want not? Sometimes a horny chick has to make do with what she has, and if he's an untouchable virgin because of his convictions, at least I'm lucky to have this. I grin at him. "'Cause I'm gonna enjoy mine."

And if his muffled curse follows me as I abandon the new game of checkers, bouncing toward the basement door, well, that's not my fault, is it?

THIRTEEN
INTERLUDE

LUCA

I have a confession to make: I'm as creepy as Kylie called me her first night at the cabin.

I sleep on the couch. I've kept the Burnses' room off-limits, even when Kylie comes upstairs to eat meals with me in the kitchen, play checkers, *chat*, and watch movies on the big television in the living room.

But every night after I'm sure Kylie is sleeping on the cot? I sneak down as quietly as possible, missing the fourth stair that I've discovered creaks, and plop my ass on the cement floor so that I can at least watch her slumber peacefully without her knowing that her captor wants her desperately.

I don't touch her, though my fingers itch to remember just how soft her skin is. I keep my distance, and if she snuffles, I hop up and hide in the bathroom until I'm sure she's fast asleep again.

If the blanket she's using to stay warm shifts in her sleep, I'll adjust it so she's covered. That's all.

And, okay, maybe I do steal her cucumber after she's done with it.

I told myself that it needed to be refrigerated. I only bought her the one—though I'll definitely add more to the next grocery order—and after she... finishes with it, it'll probably go bad quickly if she leaves it out. That's not even thinking about what's on it, or what kind of bacteria could grow, and...

And...

And I didn't put it in the refrigerator.

Because I'm a creep.

Because I'm screwing this all up.

Because I'm her captor, and I'm supposed to make her love me.

But, most of all, I'm fucked because, somehow, I'm the one falling for her.

It's undeniable. It's not just how attracted I am to her, though that's just as hard to ignore. It's been days... *days*... and I can honestly say that she is the most interesting person I've ever met in my life. She doesn't react in any way that I would expect, and she seems to find a secret humor in *everything*.

I drug her? Kidnap her? She shrugs it off. I hide her away in the basement? She helpfully reminds me that I need to keep the door locked. I buy her clothes, and she puts on a fashion show for me so I know that I got the right size.

And when I buy her a cucumber because I'm trying my best to trick her into forming a bond with me, she washes it, then shows me exactly what she's going to use it for.

I almost followed her downstairs. Every nerve in my body was singing with arousal and anticipation. I haven't been able to control my cock around her at all. I'm hard constantly, but when she gave me a glimpse of her pussy just now?

I nearly came then and there.

Tasting her musk from the cucumber? Fuck yeah, I didn't just eat it. I licked that fucker, and I'd do it again. It's the closest I'll get to Kylie—for now, at least—and I'm simping so hard, it's at least *something*.

Just like my shower time is.

I've gotta be the squeakiest-clean motherfucker on the mountain. It's a good thing that I turn the knob all the way to the right to make the spray as cold as possible otherwise Kylie wouldn't have any warm water for her own. I'm in the upstairs shower stall at least four times a day so that I can grab my cock, jerk it to thoughts of Kylie, and let the jizz run down the drain with the water.

Stripping quickly, I hop into the chilly shower spray now, hoping that might help the heat coursing through me when I think of Kylie and her cucumber.

My cock is heavy, jutting outward, nearly jumping into my waiting palm.

The cold water doesn't do shit to shake the lust controlling me. The only thing that will is the pop of pleasure as I chase my orgasm and nut all over the porcelain beneath my feet.

And that's exactly what I do. Bracing one hand against the wall, bowing my head under the spray so that it hits me in the back, I fuck my fist.

I'm right-handed. My parents knew what they were doing when they chose my right arm to leave their mark. Every time I pump my fist, stroking myself off, I can't help but look at the mess my forearm is and remember their rules.

No masturbating was one I fought as long as I could, and one of the reasons my arm looks the way it does. The devil made dirty boys touch themselves, my mother told me. The devil needed to go...

I didn't just lose the devil in my soul. I tracked him down myself, and now I wear his mark on my bicep. Like the slashes Cross tattooed near my scar, it's a way for me to shuck off the chains that my parents and their fucking cult shackled me with long before I had any choice.

I watch the ruined skin ripple slightly as the need slithers down to the base of my spine. My whole body tightens. I dig into the tiles on the wall, bracing my feet against the slick floor as I twist the head of my cock, semen spurting out in thick, ropy jets that mingle with the water welling up under me as I grit out the word, "*Fuck*."

It makes my climax even more powerful knowing that, a floor below, Kylie might be doing the same exact thing with her fingers...

thou shall not...

FOURTEEN
YES

KYLIE

My cucumber is... missing?

To be fair, once I slept off the orgasm I gave myself, I completely forgot about the poor vegetable.

Fruit?

Shit. How does that work? Seeds make something a fruit, and cucumbers have seeds. But they're also green and not sweet at all so doesn't that make them a vegetable?

Whatever.

I forgot all about it, and when I remembered that I should probably dispose of it, it was gone. Figuring it rolled off the stupid cot I have to sleep on, I checked underneath it. Nope. There was no sign of it at all, and

I just hoped I found out where it went before it started to get moldy and stunk up the basement.

It's bad enough that the contained space sure as hell smelled of pussy when I was done. To take the cuke as far inside of me as I did, stretching me out just enough for the pressure to help me go off as I flicked my clit, I still needed to produce a shit ton of natural lubricant. I was dripping *everywhere*.

Too bad Luca didn't want to play.

Shit. Saving himself... if I have to be stuck in a mountain cabin with a guy as good-looking as Luca St. James, why couldn't he be a player? Or a manwhore? Someone who would have no problem throwing my ankles up by my ears and fucking me senseless?

That cuke helped, but when I thought about how much better it is to have a warm dick inside of me, attached to a man with fingers and lips and hypnotic green eyes instead of a clammy green peel...

Damn it. I want Luca. Can't have him, but I want him, and after a couple of days torturing myself with how fucking hot I am for him—and still not being able to locate the cuke—I decide to see if we got more in with the latest grocery order.

I didn't plan on asking him if he had any idea what happened to the last one. It was embarrassing to admit that I revved us both up by playing with myself in front of Luca only for him to stay upstairs, leaving me and the cucumber alone downstairs to finish what I started. Then, to add insult to injury, I lost the stupid thing.

So I didn't mention it after the fact. Following my lead, Luca didn't bring up the cucumber, either. We just went back to watching random movies on the streaming service Luca's buddy is logged into after I told Luca that I was sick and tired of losing at checkers.

Of course, he challenged me to one last game. I won it so easily that it was obvious he *let* me win, and while I appreciated the gesture, that took all the fun out of it. Besides, having an excuse to snuggle up next to Luca on the couch... I'm fucking shameless. I'll take it, even if he won't let me take him.

I've earned some freedom. He's always upstairs. The cabin proper has four rooms: one that belongs to his buddy, a bathroom, the kitchen, and the living room. We don't go in his friend's bedroom; well, Luca doesn't. I've gotten used to the bathroom in the basement. The kitchen is for meals and our checker games. The living room is where the TV and the fireplace are.

No matter where I am, Luca can tell that I'm there. I'm still locked in the basement every night, but during the day when he's awake? He lets me stay upstairs. I've proven that I'm not going to run for the front door given the chance, and he's stopped treating me like a captive.

Not like he ever really did. But it's... it's different now. We're kind of like two people who met on vacation, got snowe-in together, and had no choice but to get along—and get to know each other—until we can leave again.

There's snow on the mountain. It's not enough to keep us trapped here, as much as I'd like to pretend otherwise. I know our days are dwindling down. Luca's been receiving phone calls daily from the Sinners. He goes outside each time, but when he stays by the door, I can overhear enough to know that Devil's ready for him to come back—with or without the liability.

Me. I'm the liability.

I ignore all that. I'm not ready to give up Luca yet. Not ready to poison him and leave him buried in the icy snow out back. I could. I mean, I've peeked outside once or twice. Luca even let us go on a walk around the cabin, showing off the wintry mountain.

That's how I know that same town car is out there. Plus, there's enough space behind the cabin to bury dozens of bodies with room to spare.

And, no, that's not a morbid thought at all. That's just the Hummingbird peeking through...

I like not having to be the Hummingbird. I know I'll have to return to the real world soon, but until I *have* to, I'm gonna get my kicks while I can.

Including just how devious I am when I ask Luca about a new shipment of cucumbers, and instead of simply admitting they haven't been delivered yet, he looks super fucking shady as he explains that he's been trying to replace mine but he hasn't been able to.

Sorry, but I jump on the word 'replace'.

"Replace? What happened to the other one?"

He blinks. "What do you mean?"

"What I said, ace." I arch my eyebrow at him. "Where's my cuke?"

"I... ate it."

"Did you at least peel it first?" Luca flushes, and I can't help but laugh. "Oh, you've got a kinky side, don't you? I never would've guessed."

His flush deepens. "No. Not kinky. Just repressed."

I stifle my laugh. He sounds so flat when he says that, it's not as funny as it was two seconds ago.

He's so repressed that he refuses to allow himself to be sexual with another person, but he... what? Tortures himself by watching me get my own rocks off, then somehow gets his hands on my used cucumber to *snack* on?

I shouldn't tease. That's just being cruel.

Especially when he admits softly, "It's not as easy as I make it look, abstaining the way that I do."

Well, that's a problem easily solved.

Scooting so that our thighs are touching on the couch, I run my fingers over his arm. "So don't. I mean, if you're ready to fuck, I can't think of a better way to spend our time while your boss decides whether to kill me or not."

His cheeks hollow.

Hm. Was it something I said?

Oh. Right. Probably my multiple blatant propositions to fuck him. Or, you know, the way I can't keep myself from reminding him that we're only together in the cabin because the Devil of Springfield wants me dead, but Luca offered to watch me and somehow convince me that I didn't see shit that night instead...

I take my hand back. "Sorry. I know better than to be a pushy bitch. You said you were waiting, and I respect that. Your religion is obviously important to you"—even though it seems hypocritical to me that he's a *gangster*, but whatever—"and how you deal with it is your thing. I'll be good. Promise."

I took my hand back—and he shoots his out, laying it on top of me, twisting my wrist gently so that he can intertwine my fingers with his.

My breath catches.

"The other day, you wanted to see what's under my sleeve."

I did. "Uh-huh."

He takes a deep breath, shuddering it out. "Okay. You can look—"

I want to, but now I'm not so sure I should. "Luca..."

"It's okay. If anything, it might help you understand why I'm so fucking twisted up inside. Because... *fuck*. I want you, Kylie. Don't ever doubt that. Those glimpses you've given me... I don't give a shit if I *am* sinning. I mean, I'm a Sinner, right? But before I was a Sinner, I grew up in a church that really screwed me up. Inside and out. Go on. I mean it."

How can I refuse?

Still holding his hand, I use the other one to shove his sleeve up to the crook of his elbow.

And then I see motherfucking *red*.

I look at life as if everything exists for my entertainment. I always have. The only time the rage wins, I do things so incredibly reckless, they change my life forever. That's why I've learned to control my anger, taking the world as a big joke.

But when I look at this—

"Kylie?"

Shit. I'm squeezing his hand so tightly, I've jabbed my nails in his skin. Good job, idiot. Why not hurt this poor man some more?

Quickly, I untangle our fingers, dropping my hand in my lap. It's either that or run my fingertips over the bumps to see if his skin feels as hard and lumpy as it looks.

He's covered in an old, pink scar. That much is obvious. Stretching nearly the whole length of his forearm, I can tell exactly why he's been hiding this from me. Because it's not just a scar.

It's a *brand*.

Those are third-degree burns that just healed wrong. I get the idea that that was on purpose. Someone branded him with a Christian cross, sizzling his skin until it bubbled up and turned into this horrifying mark.

Underneath the left part of the shorter side of the cross, I see four lines intersected with a fifth. Under the right part, there are three more. Those are obviously tattoos, done in black ink. I don't know what they mean, and I barely pay them any attention since I'm too disturbed by the terrible brand.

Finally ripping my gaze away from it, swallowing the fury that has me trembling in place, I look at Luca.

His expression is blank.

"Did Devil do that?"

If he did, he's a *dead* man.

"My parents did it," he says, his tone as emotionless as I've ever heard it. "Using fire and an iron that they just so happened to have to brand their only son."

I don't even know how to react—until Luca's voice turns sad. "'Burn the devil out of the boy'," he mumbles, and there is only one reaction *to* have.

I hiss through my teeth: "I'll fucking *kill* them."

His head shoots up. Both of his eyebrows go sky-high. "What was that?"

Shit. Fun-time Kylie doesn't get murderous. And since Luca can't know that I'm the Hummingbird...

I shake my head, sending my loose curls dancing around my face. "Nothing. I just... what the fuck, Luca? Why would they do that to you?"

He moves his arm so that I can see it from his angle. "Look at it this way. It's upside down, right? You know what that means?" I shake my head again, and he tells me, "It's the mark of Satan, they said. Bullshit. Anyone raised in a Christian church knows it's the Cross of Saint Peter. But the prophet who ruled our sect insisted that those teachings were wrong. That the symbol is anti-Christian and satanic. My parents agreed." He huffs, shaking out his arm. "Even though they branded the cross the right-side up when they were looking at it, they claimed the devil's influence was working on me even more once the mark was on my skin. When the prophet said I had to go, they agreed. The cross didn't take, they said, and then they disowned me."

The fire inside me rages higher. I still want to kill them—and this prophet, too—but I know better than to say so out loud again.

Instead, I just stay quiet.

Luca is glancing down at the burn. "They thought I was working with the devil. That I was a demonic son. Look at me now, Kylie. I am."

What? "You're not demonic, Luca. You're *good*."

"Maybe. But I do work for the Devil of Springfield. I wanted to. I *begged* him for a job. I told him about my years as a wheelman in Hamilton, but you know what he did? He brushed me off. Didn't need a driver, he said. But then he saw this mark on me by accident... and, suddenly, he was passing me the keys. I've been working for him ever since. I've been loyal to Devil ever since. You need to understand that, Kylie. I'll do anything for the boss."

I don't doubt that for a second.

"What about these?" I ask. Luca reminding me that we're only in this situation on Devil's orders isn't helping me rein in my anger. I need another distraction. I stroke one of the black line tattoos with my pointer finger. "Did your parents give you these, too?"

"Nah. This was me taking ownership of the way they ruined my arm. I mean, if they could disfigure it with a scar, why not get a tattoo? Working for Devil, I knew I would wear his mark on my skin. But these..." He counts them out. "Eight. The prophet had a hundred rules for us, but I believed in the Commandments. I got a mark for each time I willingly broke one."

He has eight, which means there are two he hasn't broken yet.

I only know, like, the four main ones. It's easier for me to ask him which ones he's missing than try to figure them out myself.

Somehow, I'm not even a little surprised when he answers my curiosity with: "Thou shall not kill. Thou shall not commit adultery."

Funny, thou shall not fuck a woman who's into you —and that you're into, too—isn't one of them...

They brainwashed him. That's the long and short of it. This prophet and his garbage parents... they did a number on this poor guy. And now he's sitting on the couch with me after admitting that he chowed down on the cucumber I fucked in a way to get around the brainwashing that he hasn't shucked as much as he thinks he has.

Poor Luca. Repressed isn't the half of it.

I can't make his scars go away. Not the physical one

on his arm, or the ones that have hurt him deep inside. Just like I am, Luca was broken before I ever met him, but I'm here now.

The Hummingbird's first instinct is to find his parents and kill them for hurting this kind-hearted, sweet man.

Kylie's?

I think of the cucumber, and even if using sex to distract him isn't something that Luca is used to, I also know that there are some things he's open to...

I tap his knee. "So... the cucumber. Was it tasty?"

For a moment, he looks confused. Like he has no idea where the sudden change in topic came from. "Kylie?"

C'mon, Luca. Play along. "Did you *like* it?"

His nostrils flare. "I... it was delicious. It was delicious because it was yours."

Good boy. "Really? I'm glad. But you know what's better?"

"What?" he grates out.

I grin. "Tasting it straight from the source."

Luca freezes for a moment, then a dark look shadows his face. "I didn't tell you all that so you could pity me, Kylie. I did it so you understand. For twenty-one years I was raised one way. I've been working to shake it off for so long now, and while these marks stand for how far I've come... I can't go all the way yet."

Literally.

I purse my lips. "Pity you?" I say. "Shit, ace, if I was pitying you, I'd offer to suck your dick."

He sucks in a breath.

A thought occurs to me. I know he's a virgin, but when he says he's saving himself for marriage, does that mean just penetrative sex? Or all sex?

I nudge his thigh. "If I did, would I be the first?"

He shakes his head.

Damn it. I don't realize how much I like the idea of being Luca's first *anything* until he admits that someone's been intimate with his dick before I've had the chance.

Okay. "How about if I let you go down on me? Have you done that before?"

This time he answers me with a very throaty, "No."

"Do you want to?"

When Luca stays silent, I cover my renewed rejection with a casual shrug as I start to get up from the couch. "If you change your mind, you know where to find me."

I've taken two steps before he says, "Yes."

I spin around to look at him. "Yes, you know where to find me?"

He shakes his head. "I mean, yes, I want to know what you taste like."

Okay, then.

thou shall not...

FIFTEEN
CONFESSION

KYLIE

I don't want to give Luca any time to overthink and change his mind.

Now, if he revokes consent at any point? He wants to stop? We stop. But if the only thing stopping him from getting me off is the voices in his head telling a twenty-seven-year-old man that sex is dirty and bad and wrong, then fuck that. I want him. He seems to want me.

Let's go.

As uncomfortable as the cot is, it's wider than the couch. I want to be able to stretch out and not have to worry about rolling off if we get too into it. Once I point that out, Luca agrees, and the two of us head down to the basement together.

To be fair, I could snap a collar around his neck,

lead him on a leash, and he'd follow me wherever I wanted him to go. The idea that I'm willing to let him eat me out has him nearly tripping over his feet on the way down, he's that eager. Me? I'm so wet, I'm surprised I'm not squelching as my thighs rub together on the way down.

Once we're there, I start shimmying off my leggings. I stopped wearing boots around the cabin because it helped Luca realize that I'm not about to run out into the snow in my sock-covered feet. I see another perk in that I don't have to waste any time unlacing my boots and shucking them. Oh, no. I just kick off my leggings, sending them flying while I reach for my panties.

They're the next to go, and as Luca watches my frantic motions with lust mingled with desire, I hop on one foot, then the other, until I'm completely naked from the waist down.

I jump on top of the bed, landing on my knees in my haste and my excitement. Flipping to my back, I scoot my bare ass against the rumpled sheet until I'm up against the headboard. I wrap my hands around two of the bars to give me something to hold onto.

Then, angling my body so that I'm in a comfortable position, I spread my legs wide open and tell Luca, "Whenever you're ready, ace."

His tongue darts out, swiping over the corner of his mouth. His eyes are locked on my open legs.

On my pussy.

He breathes in deep. "I've never seen one open like that in the flesh before."

"You sure you can handle me?" I ask. I mean for it to be more of a seductive tease, but my voice cracks just enough to be noticeable.

"Here's something else you can learn about me," Luca tells me, taking one step toward me, then another. "I'm a very fast learner. I was homeschooled. They didn't teach me shit about the real world. I've had to learn it on my own. Books help. Going online helps. Videos... I'm a very visual learner." The bed dips as he presses one knee to the mattress. "And I've watched a ton of porn."

I giggle. "I'm sure your prophet wouldn't be happy hearing that."

"Probably not. Then again, he might not even know what porn is. We didn't have computers in Donovan. I had to make up for a lot of lost time." He grabs my ankle, moving me slightly so that he can fit his body between my legs. "So I might not have done this before, but I'm a pro at watching other guys do it."

Using my other foot, I nudge him in the shoulder. "Just so you know, real life's not like porn. Even if I gave a shit about shaving, there's no razor here. I've got a bush."

His eyes light up. "I know."

"And some guys think it's unpleasant."

"I won't be one of them," he vows.

I don't want to talk him out of this. He seems sure,

and I am loving this cocky side of him. But at the same time, I don't know if my overinflated sense of ego will ever recover if he hates it. "You sure about that, ace?"

"I already know that I like your taste," Luca reminds me. "Besides, I don't want to go down on a porn star. I want to go down on *you*."

Before I can even give him a smart-ass reply—something like, *what are you waiting for then*—Luca bows down in front of my pussy, burying his face in my damp curls.

He might not have the experience when it comes to giving head, but he makes up for it with enthusiasm. He wasn't kidding when he said he would like my taste. My guy is slurping down there, and I might actually be a little embarrassed myself at how fucking wet I am if it wasn't obvious that he's having the time of his life.

He licks. Sucks. Nuzzles. I can't imagine how much hair he's dealing with, plucking loose, getting in his teeth, but if it's bothering him, you'd never know. In fact, when he isn't using his tongue to gather up every drop I'm producing, he uses his teeth to nibble along my labia.

One hand is digging into my thigh as I start bucking against his motions. His other hand is grabbing me by the hood, holding me open so that he could target my clit.

I squeeze the bars, grunting and panting and holding on for dear life as he refuses to do anything but focus all of his attention on making me come.

Every now and then, though, he comes up for air, almost as though he's checking to make sure that he's doing all right, but when I snap his name, he goes right back to making me feel fucking *amazing*.

He blows a hot rush of air on my pussy.

"Do that again," I order.

He does.

I throw my head back. "No way," I pant. "No way this is your first time."

He nuzzles me again. "Told you, baby. I'm a quick learner."

Baby? Know what? In this moment, while I'm seconds away from climaxing, I'll be whatever the fuck he wants me to be...

"Of course, it helps that it's you. I swear to fucking God, there's nowhere I'd rather be than between these thighs," he murmurs, and I gasp as I get Luca St. James to blaspheme. "Fuck, you taste delicious. I knew you would."

I want to remind him that he already got a hint when he ate the cucumber, but he uses his teeth to scrape my clit and, whoopsie, all I can manage is a high-pitched squeal in response.

"That feel good?"

My throat is raw from the squeal. "You know it did. Keep going. I'm so fucking close."

He stops.

If I had my knife nearby, I might've stabbed him.

"What the fuck? Didn't you hear me? I said keep going."

Unless—

Unless he wants to stop.

Damn it!

I release the bars. "You suck, dude. Get me all worked up, then stop right in front of the finish line."

"What? No. *No*, baby. I'm not stopping."

He isn't? I'm not so sure about that since he's climbing up from his place between my thighs. And look... now he's gesturing for me to... to...

"What? Why do you want me to get up?"

"Just do it."

Whoa. I've never had Luca be so forceful with me before... and I *like* it.

He wants me up? Sure. I can do that.

My legs shaky, my lower gut tight and achy from unfulfilled need, I push myself up and off of the bed.

As soon as I'm standing, Luca drops down on the bed himself, flat on his back. "Okay. I'm ready. Sit on me."

Oh. *Oh*.

"Are you kidding? You want to suffocate, ace?"

"I can't think of a better way to go," he says earnestly, tapping his shoulders. "But if I'm only going to experience this once, I'm going to make this something for both of us to remember. Put your knees there. I want your full pussy on my face."

I don't know why he thinks this is a one-and-done.

For as long as we're here, I don't see why we can't do this again and again and—

I must've reacted too slowly for him. Before I know it, he's sitting up, grabbing my hand, tugging me back onto the bed. Once I'm there, he shifts his hold, hefting me up by the waist and dropping me right on top of his face like he wanted.

In this position, Luca almost instantly finds my entrance and, I don't know how he manages it, but he curls his tongue and basically *fucks* me with it.

I don't have to worry about him suffocating after all. He just uses his tongue, leaving his nose clear to breathe until I'm squealing his name, writhing on his face, wringing every last bit of my orgasm out.

Only then, when I'm limp and sated, well-pleasured and inexplicably content, do I make sure that Luca is doing okay.

His lips are shiny with my juices. They glisten beneath the dim light in the basement as I slide down his chest so that I can face him.

Curving his arm around me, keeping me connected to him as he pushes himself up into a seated position, Luca tugs me onto his lap.

There's no escape—and, like always, nowhere I want to run to anyway.

He presses a sweet kiss to my cheek. "Thank you," he whispers huskily against my sweat-slicked skin.

No, Luca. Thank *you*.

He looks dazed. Almost as though he got *more*

enjoyment than I did. As if kissing my pussy is all he's ever wanted to do...

He kissed my pussy. My cheek, too.

Laying my hand on his cheek, I close the gap between us, pressing my lips to his.

I immediately taste myself on his mouth. I could give a fuck. Right now, all I want to do is find some intimacy with Luca, and since he's not ready for what I want, I give him what I need.

I kiss him.

His kiss is as charmingly awkward as it is eager, and that makes it even more special when it's done.

I hear his swallow in the sudden quiet before he whispers, "You didn't have to do that."

Right. Like he didn't have to make me go off like a rocket, right?

I curl myself up on his chest. I can't help it. I've always been my most vulnerable after sex. That's why I've stuck with one-night stands lately. There's nothing but raw attraction—or even just basic lust—when I pick out a guy, fuck him senseless, and then go on my way. Things get iffy when emotions are involved.

And, somehow, someway, emotions have gotten involved with Luca.

"There's something about you, ace..."

His arms wrap around me. I notice he was hesitant at first, but when I lay my head against him, he completes the circle.

I can't see his face. That makes it so much easier to

tell him things I wouldn't have if that hadn't just happened. "I know you can't help but wonder why I'm okay staying here. The truth is, I've been bouncing from place to place for years now. For work... to get away from my family's expectations for me... I've just been gone. But now... you make me want to settle down."

There. I'm attracted to Luca. I wish it was just sex, but it's never been just sex with him. It's the way he takes care of me, no matter why he does. It's how good he seems, and how his biggest rebellion against a fucked-up childhood is getting a tattoo and breaking archaic church doctrine.

"I should hate you for it," I murmur. "I should hate you for keeping me here, but I think we both know I could leave anytime I want. Sure, Devil would shoot me—"

He squeezes me. "I wouldn't let him."

My laugh is hollow. "You're only saying that because I just rode your face like a fucking cowgirl."

I jostle, and it takes me a second to realize that I am because he's shaking his head so roughly, the motion travels down his body. "It's not just that. You said there's something about me? Well, there's something about you." He rests his forehead against the side of my head. "I asked him if I could have you. That's the truth for me, baby. I saw you... I wanted you. Not just because I didn't want to see Devil kill you. I watch Devil kill all the time. But you... you were different." A sigh, and then another confession: "I want to keep you."

That's enough to have me pushing against him, breaking against his hold so that I can see the serious-ness written in every line of his face. "And what? Marry me so that you can fuck me? Is that your endgame?"

He's quiet. Holy shit! Maybe I am being too emotional right now, but I think he would. This man I barely know would marry me just so we could fuck.

As much as you'd think otherwise, it's never just been about sex to me. Is that what it is for Luca?

If so...

"You don't have to get married to have sex," I tell him firmly.

It would be so much easier if he agreed. Only he doesn't. He just mutters, "*I* do," and I know he's not doing it to be a wise ass. He means it. He's really going to wait until he's married.

I think about it for a second. "When you say 'sex', we're talking PIV, right? Dick in pussy? What we just did... that didn't count?"

It's his turn to mull over my words. "Right."

"If you got me another cucumber and fucked me with it? Still good?"

His answer comes quicker this time. "Yes."

I have one more question for him: "Are you ready to let me go?"

This is the longest pause. Finally, he says, "I don't know if you noticed earlier, but it was beginning to snow... the weather forecast calls for four to six inches. It wouldn't be safe to drive down the mountain in that. Plus, Christmas is in two days. You told me you don't really care about it. I have no plans... we can spend it up here, watching the snow fall and sitting in front of the fire."

And maybe doing some of those things I mentioned that don't break Luca's promise to himself...

"When you put it like that, I guess we'll be sticking around a little longer."

I just wonder how much longer it will be.

thou shall not...

SIXTEEN
CHRISTMAS GIFT

LUCA

Kylie doesn't know it, but I'm planning on forever.

I know it's soon. I know I don't deserve a girl like her. I don't care. Apart from convincing Devil to hire me on as his personal driver, I never get what I want.

That changes now.

I have at least two more days to make her fall in love with me. I haven't been trying, not really, since it seemed so disingenuous at first. I wanted to make her love me in a bid to save her life. Sure. That's what I told myself then.

I know better.

From the moment I first looked into her pretty brown eyes, I think I knew that she was it for me. So different from Emily in every way, I actually instinctively recognized that that was a plus. I wasn't looking to replace my childhood sweetheart. I could've already if that's all I wanted.

No. I want Kylie, and I'm going to do everything I can to keep her.

The timing couldn't be better. It's Christmas. I was aware of that going into this when I did everything I could to get Devil to let me keep her until her blabbing about the vice mayor's murder was no longer a threat to the Sinners Syndicate. If it wasn't quick, and the boss didn't pull the op immediately, the craziness of the holiday season meant that most people would be too busy to wonder where I was, and what was happening with Kylie, without checking in on my progress all the time.

I got lucky in more ways than one. For now, the straight-and-narrow cops aren't looking at Devil for Collins's murder. Rumors of that hitman have taken hold in Springfield, plus Mayor Harrison—on Devil and Libellula's orders—is doing his best to downplay his second's untimely demise.

If it was anyone else but a high-profile politician in Springfield, none of this would've had to happen. How many men has Devil eliminated, whether personally or on his orders? The DA is always trying to get him on gun charges, plus sex trafficking. Murder? He's as clean as a man can be with his rep.

Of course, that's because of Rolls. That man and his

crew can disappear anyone, but the vice mayor's body *needed* to be found. Not only because there's a witness being held captive by the Sinners, but because Collins's brutal death was a message to one man: Johnny Winter.

He hasn't come out of hiding yet. Devil thought he might, but it seems like the Hummingbird rumors must've confused Winter. Instead of coming after Devil because he offed one of his bought informants, he's been putting out feelers, searching for the Hummingbird.

No one can find that guy, either.

Luckily, that means Devil gave the go-ahead to stay on the mountain with Kylie a little longer. At least through Christmas, and if shit doesn't change one way or another, then possibly up until after New Year's, too.

I'm trying not to get too ahead of myself. Of course, when Kylie is sleeping and I'm watching the peaceful, snuffling snores as they escape her, I imagine a future where she pledges her loyalty to me, to Devil, to the Sinners before she agrees to marry me and, yes, I finally allow myself to fuck her.

Those are fantasies, though. Secret, dark, and twisted thoughts I hold close since that's about as much affection as I've had since the night she invited me between her thighs, and I greedily accepted.

No. Sorry. That's not true. After she kissed me— and I creamed in my pants when I finally lost control of the erection I'd been fighting the entire time I was feasting on her delicious pussy—she was the softest, most sweetest thing I've ever seen. She didn't let me go upstairs. Instead, she all but pleaded with me to stay down in the basement with her.

The cot had room for two if we squeezed, she pointed out. And after she let me fuck her with my mouth, it didn't feel right to just go upstairs to an empty couch.

So I laid down with her. We slept—actually slept— and I had my first fully peaceful night in... well, *forever*.

I need that. I crave it.

I'll do anything to have it.

I'm taking each day as it comes, though. The next morning, Kylie went back to her bubbly yet notably snarky self. She didn't mention any of her murmured confessions from the night before. Following her lead, I stayed quiet myself.

Confession... that's exactly what it reminded me of. Like when the prophet called you up to his pulpit and wouldn't let you leave it until you admitted your deepest, darkest sins... and then, when you walked away, you wondered if you should have said anything at all.

I wonder if Kylie regrets what she said.

What we *did*.

I can't ask her. It'll fucking kill me if she does. So, rather than face the reality that I'm living in denial— and delusion—I simply did everything I could to give her a Christmas Eve that suited us both.

The fire in the fireplace burned. We watched

Rudolph the Red-Nosed Reindeer and all of the *Santa Clause* movies. We don't have a tree, obviously, or any decorations, but while Kylie poked at the steaks I ordered specifically for our dinner, I went out into the snow. By the time she realized I had slipped outside, I was back, and I picked enough branches off of one of the evergreen pines outside to scatter in front of the fire, filling the cabin with the scent of Christmas.

We started out on opposite sides of the couch that morning. By the time our Christmas Eve together was over, she was snuggling next to me. Actually, she fell asleep nestled up against me, her hand splayed on my chest, her head resting on my bicep.

Like always, I watched her sleep until my own eyes got drowsy. Easing out of her snuggle, I got up, turned the fireplace off, then picked Kylie up in a bridal-style carry so I could bring her to the cot in the basement.

It hit me then that it was nearly the same thing that I did two weeks ago when I first brought her to Burns's cabin. She was sedated last time so I could move more quickly. Now? I refuse to disturb her rest. It takes twice as long to carry her downstairs. Once I have, I lay her out on the cot.

No chains this time. No handcuffs. I just tuck her in off to the furthest side of the cot before climbing in next to her.

It's the best Christmas Eve I've ever had.

Christmas is just as magical.

I wake up, reaching out for Kylie, my heart jumping into my throat when my hand slides across the cool sheet. My body realized that she was missing a split second before my brain did. Unfortunately, that meant it was already moving before the panic hit me, resulting in all five foot-eleven inches of me rolling off the bed, landing face-first on the concrete floor.

Fuck.

"Kylie?" With my face mashed against the floor, it comes out muffled. Shaking off the fall, I push up until I'm on my knees. "Kylie!"

No answer.

It's Christmas. She wouldn't have left. She has to be here. But where the hell did she go? She's never left me alone in the basement before, and as I scrabble up, rushing for the stairs, I prepare myself to find the door locked.

I'll kick that fucker down if I have to. My sneakers were left in the living room, but I don't care. I'll break a foot if that's what it takes.

Nothing will keep me from going after her.

Good thing that my brain went fully back online in the seconds before I reached the top of the stairs. I might've kicked through damn air since the door leading down to the basement is *open*.

I haul myself up the final three steps, landing on the living room floor in a half-crouch as I call her name again.

"Kylie!"

"In here, ace."

Thank fucking God.

My head whips around. Kylie is standing in the kitchen, holding a spatula, wearing one of the over-sized t-shirts I bought her. They come in a 5-pack, and when she told me she preferred to sleep in them when she wasn't sleeping naked, I got the t-shirts because, *shit*, this woman really is temptation personified.

And she's here.

She didn't leave me.

I jog right to her side, sweeping her up in a hug so tight, she starts slapping me in the back with the spatula.

I can't let her go. Not yet. So I give her one last squeeze, then set her back down on her bare feet.

She cocks her hip, smirking up at me as she does. "Let me guess. You woke up. Saw I was gone. Lost all your shit, and now you're glad I didn't escape so you won't have to hunt me down for Devil?"

Something like that.

Except, perhaps, for the Devil part...

I RUN MY FINGERS NERVOUSLY THROUGH MY HAIR. "THAT obvious?"

With her free hand, Kylie holds her pointer finger and her thumb about an inch apart. "A smidge."

"Sorry."

"Don't be. You looked like you were enjoying your rest. I figured... since it's the holiday and all... I should let you sleep in. Let you enjoy it. Look. I made breakfast."

She did. There are scrambled eggs in the pan on the stove, plus a couple of slices of bacon resting on a piece of paper towel.

I breathe in deep. "It smells delicious."

"Hold that thought. My eggs usually come out rubbery as hell, but I tried."

As she plates them, I goose her in the side, then take a seat. "Is this my Christmas present?"

She raises an eyebrow at me. "We just met, ace. You think we're doing presents?"

Oh. "Well..."

Kylie laughs. The sound soothes the last of the pain lingering from when I slammed into the floor. "Holy shit. I should've known better. You got me a present, didn't you?"

"It's not wrapped or anything," I tell her. "And it's not something pricey like jewelry. But... it's Christmas. I wanted to get you *something*."

She shakes her head. "Why am I not surprised? You're always giving me presents, ace. Told you. You need to stop in case I get attached."

That's exactly what I'm hoping for.

I start to rise up. "I can go get it—"

"No," she says, cutting me off as she slips a plate in front of me. "Eat first. I can wait."

If she says so.

I drop my ass back into the seat, reaching for the fork. However, I barely scoop up some of the admittedly overcooked eggs onto it before I notice that I'm the only one with a plate. "Aren't you eating?"

I expect her to say she already did while I was sleeping, but she doesn't. She just shakes her head.

I don't like that. "You barely touched your steak last night, either. What's the matter? Not hungry?"

She snorts. "Oh, no. I'm fucking starving. But I know better than to have a big meal right now. Not until I give you my gift."

My whole body warms. "I get something, too?" I *never* get gifts... "What is it?"

"Me."

Shit. Did I say my whole body warmed? It's on fucking fire at just the idea of what Kylie could mean by that. Will I get to taste her pussy again? Do I get to keep her? Is there something else we can try?

My cock seems to pulse. I already had morning wood to deal with, but it deflated in the fear that I let Kylie slip out from between my fingers. It comes roaring back to life, though I grit my teeth to hide just how much I want whatever she's offering to give me.

I fuck up. She sees my grimace and immediately feels like she has to explain.

"Hear me out. You said it only counts if you fuck a pussy. Your mouth on me didn't count. If I sucked you off, it would be the same. I figure, by your logic, then my ass doesn't count, either. If you want to fuck without breaking your promise, that might work."

I drop my fork, my body electric with the promise of finding out what any part of Kylie feels like wrapped around my dick.

"I did the best I could to prep," she continues, "so that it's not as messy as it normally would be. I'm okay with eating after if this is something you want to try."

I finally find my voice. "But won't it hurt?" I can't imagine shoving anything up my ass... "I won't hurt you, Kylie."

"You won't. Look." She gets up from her seat, nearly bouncing to the other side of the kitchen. When she returns, she has a large bottle of a viscous-looking clear liquid. "It's lube," she announces. "I found this in the bathroom downstairs when we first arrived, and I thought of it when I came up with the idea the other day. Oh, and side note: your friend who owns this place? Between the shit I found under the sink and the chains, he's a full-on freak. You know that?"

I'm beginning to think that, after this, I'll never look at Burns the same way again. "I know."

"Lucky for us anyway. With my limited prep and the lube, it should work. Of course, feel free to say 'no'. It was just a thought—"

"Yes."

Kylie's lips curve at my easy acquiescence. "There might be shit."

"Don't care."

"You'll have to go easy. I'm trusting you not to take advantage when I'm under you."

Pushing away my chair from the table, I snarl, "I would *never*."

"Oh. I know," she says, waving her hand, making the lubricant slosh. "I just wanted to make that clear. So... if you really want to do it, I'd prefer getting started. You might not want those eggs, but they're looking pretty good to me now."

She made them for me. It takes me six bites as I loom over the edge of the table, devouring each one of them. I chow down on the bacon, showing her my clean plate.

She giggles. "I guess I can make more."

"I'll cook for you," I promise. "Later." I reach for her, taking her hand. "The cot?"

She nods. "That's what I was thinking."

I start to pull her toward the entrance that leads out of the kitchen and into the living room. But then I stop. "Wait. Your gift—"

"Is it a condom? Because that's the only thing I couldn't find in your buddy's room."

Of course not. Officer Burns fuck his wife with any protection? That man is so obsessed with the lovely brunette who runs the flower shop, I'm surprised he hasn't knocked her up the way that Devil did to Ava.

"No." I pause. "You want me to ruin the surprise?"

"Go ahead, ace."

"I got you a blow dryer and a... what's it called?

Diffuser thing? You kept saying it was a pain in the ass for your curls to air dry. So I got you that."

Her eyes light up. "Good choice. But, yeah. That can wait. Especially since all I want for Christmas is to find out what you've been hiding in your jeans."

It would be my pleasure.

My heart is pounding the entire way back to the basement. My cock is so ready to burst, it's about to fuck its way out of the jeans I sleep in just to get to Kylie.

Her ass. I gulp. The beautiful, firm, luscious ass I've been dreaming of... I'm going to get to fuck it.

Christmas Eve was great, but this is going to be the best fucking Christmas *ever*.

As soon as we reach the bottom, Kylie grabs the hem of her t-shirt. She hefts it up, pulling it over her head.

My mind momentarily goes blank.

"Naked." It comes out strangled. "You're naked."

She winks. "I told you. I prepped for this."

I have no idea what any of that means, but if she's naked, then, fuck, I better get naked, too.

Kylie has already seen everything I have to hide. I've watched her eyeing the key on my chain curiously, though she hasn't brought herself to ask the meaning behind it yet. She raged over my brand, earning her a permanent place in my heart for caring about younger me as much as she did. My tally marks, too, and my devil.

In fact, she's right. The only part of me I've kept hidden—for my own good—was my cock.

That changes now.

My poor dick is so hard, I send silent apologies over to Kylie even as she squeals in approval over what she sees reaching out for her. She went to all this trouble to give me her ass as a gift, but if I last more than a minute, I'll be surprised. It's not even about fucking her, though I'd be lying if I said her loophole isn't *genius*. I want that connection with her. I want to fill her up with my come, getting a part of me as deep inside of her as she's already wormed her way into me.

Condom? Seriously? Even if Burns did keep protection in the cabin, I would've refused. I want to feel Kylie. I want to *know* Kylie.

And as she climbs on the cot, going up on her hands and knees, a bead of pre-come slicks the head of my cock.

That won't be enough. Whether she's used to getting her ass fucked or not, or if she managed to stretch herself out to get ready for this, I've watched enough anal porn to know that, without plenty of lubricant, I will hurt her.

So maybe I pour too much as I position myself behind her. Better safe than sorry, though Kylie does squirm as I slather the chilly lube up and down the crack of her ass.

"Get it in there. Make sure I'm nice and slick. It'll make it better for both of us."

"I want you to feel good," I promise.

"I will. Just... I saw that snake you've been hiding from me, ace. I know I said you can have my ass, but please don't think you can fit all that in me. Stick with, like, an inch or two for this first time, would you?"

I bend over her, pressing a kiss to the small of her back. "If it makes you happy, I'll give you just the tip, baby. Just to know what it's like."

Just to make her *mine*.

Kylie arches her back. "I think I can take a little more than the tip."

I guess we'll see.

"You ready?"

She digs her hands into the cot. "Whenever you are."

I take a deep breath, doing my best not to go off before I even get the tip inside her. Despite all the lube I applied, that actually makes it a little harder than I thought to get my cock in position. I keep slipping, and I know she's not making fun of me, but as I curse under my breath in frustration when I miss for the third time, I'm determined to at least breach the rim of her ass on the fourth time even as she giggles softly.

I do, and the moan that she trades for her laughter is almost as pleasurable to me as the vice gripping my cock.

She's tight. Super fucking tight. I start to think that there's no way I'll be able to give her any of me because the resistance is just too much. She arches again, almost as if trying to force her ass to take more of my cock, while panting softly.

My body trembles.

Hers suddenly relaxes just enough that I get about two inches inside of her. With one more push, I'm halfway in, and I don't think I could give her more if she asked for it.

Luckily, it seems to be enough.

"Yes," she groans. "Fuck, Luca. And I mean that as an expletive and an instruction. The pressure... you have no idea how... *weird* this feels. But weird in a good way," she adds quickly. "I've never been so fucking full before."

"And that's a good thing?" I grit out.

"That's a great thing. But you know what'll make it better? If you fucking *move*."

I try my best. I don't want to pull out all of the way, and for two reasons: I'm afraid of having to go through that again to seat myself; plus, I don't want to accidentally come anywhere but inside of her.

So I start rocking my hips a little. With the globes of her ass right there, I squeeze one, enjoying how soft it feels in comparison to the tight heat strangling my dick.

That was my downfall. Kylie's soft skin has always been a fascination of mine. Add that to the sensation of finally getting to fuck her? I grip her other ass cheek in time for my shallow thrusts to stutter as my orgasm climbs up my spine. My sac tightens, I let out a grunting roar, and mere minutes after I mounted my girl, I'm spilling everything I have inside of her.

She doesn't complain that it's over so quickly. She just takes my load, then folds her arms and legs, laying flat out on the cot as I finish coming. She takes my weight just as well as her ass took my cock, and I kiss her back one more time before finally pulling out.

She groans again, and it's fucking music to my ears.

Rolling to the side of the cot, I tug her on top of my chest. My limp cock falls against my inner thigh.

She's smiling at me.

I smile back.

"Merry Christmas, Kylie."

"Back atcha, ace."

thou shall not...

SEVENTEEN
KEYS

LUCA

Curled up together on the cot, both of us fresh from our recent shower, our naked legs intertwined, I have to admit that this was the best fucking Christmas I've ever had.

True, the bar was in hell, considering the prophet refused to celebrate the secular version of Christmas. I didn't get my first Christmas present until I spent a December as Devil's driver and he gave me an expensive piece I was needing for my build, plus an eye-opening bonus. And as much as I appreciated the camshaft, Kylie letting me fuck her ass with *my* shaft tops a very short list.

I know I didn't last long. As she preened in the shower, letting me rub her down with the body wash I ordered specifically for her, she admitted that she expected it to be over quickly. There's a huge difference between fucking your fist and working your dick in and out of a tight asshole. She squeezed the life and all of my come right out of me, and I barely made it ten thrusts before I was filling her up with everything I had.

If it was anyone but Kylie, I would've been mortified. I'm a twenty-seven-year-old guy in the prime of his life. I've whacked off more in the last five years than most boys do throughout their entire teens and early twenties. I thought I had control over my cock.

I was wrong.

I couldn't keep from coming. The sensations were too powerful, but she didn't make me feel like I took her prep and her generous offer for granted. Instead, she kissed my chest, pulled me toward the bathroom, and I finally got to share a shower with her.

A shower—plus, she showed me just how much she expects to get off when we're together, even if that was meant to be my Christmas gift. Instead, I got a second one when she shoved me on my chest, pushing me to my knees before hooking one leg over my shoulder so that I could eat her pussy until she came all over my face.

Between the drip from the shower and her leg hooking me in place, it was difficult to breathe, but fuck it. If I died, I died, and like I told her the first time, it would've been an amazing way to go.

I obviously didn't. Fingers threaded through my

hair, holding me against her box, I licked and sucked and nuzzled until she was screaming my name. She might not have enjoyed it as much as when I was pumping into her ass, but hell if I didn't make sure she had a merry Christmas herself before we curled up on the cot, sated and pleasured, and ready to take a nap before I made her lunch.

At least, Kylie was ready to take a nap. I thought she passed out almost immediately. Me? Unwilling to let this amazing morning come to an end *too* quickly, I twirled one of her curls around the length of my pointer finger while trying not to notice how close my cock was to her entrance.

One thrust. If I angled my body around hers just right, all it would take is one thrust, and I could have been seated inside of her pussy.

I don't. I wouldn't. Not only would I never betray Kylie's trust like that, but I haven't changed my mind. My clever girl found a way to share her body with me without breaking my promise to myself that I'd wait for marriage. If I threw it away now, what was the point?

Even if, at this moment, my lifelong conviction is wavering a little...

"Luca?" murmurs Kylie. "You still up?"

I'm not the only one—and I don't mean how Kylie's obviously awake.

Angling my hips back so that I don't poke her with my erection, I say, "Yup. You?"

She tilts her head enough that I can see her bright eyes. In the basement, there are two lights. One dimmer light we keep on around the clock so that there's always some illumination. The more powerful bulb is directly overhead, and it lights up the entire space.

It's on for now. That's okay. I can see that she's not only wide awake. I don't think she fell asleep at all.

"What's up?"

"I'm sorry. I've been meaning to ask for ages now, and I never did, but I've been staring at it ever since we climbed into bed and..." The chain around my neck bites into the back of it as she gives it a quick tug. "What is this?"

Even without asking for verification, I know she's not asking me about the chain itself. She wants to know about the key.

My first instinct is to brush her off. This isn't really a conversation I want to have after she let me see what it was like to fuck, but because she did, I can't see any way I can refuse to answer her.

And why shouldn't I? I thought I'd turn her off when she learned the truth about the brand on my arm. That didn't happen. And if I didn't want her to ever be curious about the key I usually wear tucked under my shirt, hidden out of sight, I could have removed it before she could ask.

Maybe, in some ass-backward way, I wanted her to ask.

I wanted Kylie to know.

I wanted her to care.

And, most of all, I needed to tell her about Emily. Because how can I keep from making the same mistakes with Kylie if she doesn't know about what happened before her?

I blow out a rush of air. "It's stupid," I warn her.

"It's not," she whispers back. Letting go of the key, she slides her hand up the side of my throat before rubbing her thumb along the edge of my jaw. "If it matters to you, it's not, Luca."

"You remember how I told you about the church I was raised in? About Donovan?"

"That prophet guy?"

My jaw clenches. I'm sure she can feel it. "Yeah. Him. This key belongs to him."

She's quiet for a few seconds. "Okay. Weird. Not the kind of story I was expecting, but—"

I roll onto my back, making my confession to the ceiling. "Donovan stole my girl. So I stole his key."

Kylie rises up on her elbow so that I have no choice but to see her; at least in my peripheral vision, that is. "Back up, ace. I think I missed a bit of the story."

I exhale. "It's not a fun story. When I was still a member of the church—"

"Cult."

Right. "There weren't any other girls my age. Just Emily. Emily Dallas. Her family joined the HCofJD when we were both twelve. By thirteen, I knew she

219

would be the girl I married. At fourteen, we started to date. Church-approved dating, obviously, but when we were twenty-one, the prophet said I could marry her."

"The same prophet who, uh, stole your girl?"

"Yeah." I shift so that Kylie doesn't have to touch me if she doesn't want to. "You can guess what happened. We turned twenty-one. I thought we were engaged. And then..."

And then I was told to head to the church pulpit, where I was forced to watch Jack Donovan fuck Emily on the altar while she was wearing a white dress.

A *wedding* dress.

Because she agreed to marry him instead of me.

"She's his wife now. He decided that, of all the congregation, she was the one who was holy enough to bear his heirs. Last I heard, she's had at least two of them. She seems happy, and I want that for her... Emily was sweet. A little feisty like you. But she didn't choose me."

She was supposed to.

Maybe it wasn't meant to be. Twenty-one-year-old Luca was convinced the world was ending when I lost her. I'd known Emily for almost a decade at that point, and I *did* love her. Was I *in* love, though?

Who the fuck knows? But I *do* know that the feelings I have for this woman lying next to me right now? They're undeniable.

What would I do if I saw anyone fucking Kylie?

I'd get my ninth tally mark, that's what I'd do...

Completely oblivious to how murderous she makes me feel, Kylie scoots closer—and that only firms my decision that, if anyone is going to touch, taste, and eventually fuck this woman, it'll be *me*. "So she made the wrong fucking choice. Tough luck for Emily, but I'm not complaining because I get to have fun with you. That still doesn't answer my question about the key, though."

It doesn't, does it?

"See, Donovan has this gold altar where he keeps his copy of the Bible, his gold goblet, and his cross. This key... it belongs to that altar. I stole it. I just... I told you it was stupid, but after he married Emily, it made me feel good to know that I had something of his. And I knew he probably had a spare. I knew he could get in regardless. I was still so brainwashed, I didn't even take the cross with me when my parents disowned me."

Kylie digs her fingers in the sheets on the cot between us. My mood brightens a little when I think that she might actually give a shit about how awful my parents treated me back then.

"Probably a good idea," she says after a moment. "I mean, what would you need it for? If you left the church. The key, I get. You wouldn't want to wear a cross."

Oh. She doesn't know. "It was six inches tall and covered in diamonds. It's worth a fortune."

"What? Dude! You should've taken it. They kicked you out with nothing!"

"I know. I also should've realized that no prophet, priest, or pastor would have such a fucking gaudy cross. It was a sign of how loaded he was. Of how powerful he was when it came to taking every last dime his congregation had. You were right. He *is* a cult leader." Plain and simple. "And even though I didn't take the cross, I took this key." I hold it between my forefinger and thumb. "To me, it's a reminder of what I left behind. What I escaped from. It's also a sign that I'll never go back."

Reaching up, Kylie's soft fingers ghost over the bumpy brand on my forearm. "This should've been the first one, ace."

"I know. And it is. I needed it, too."

"What do you mean?"

She wants to know? I'll tell her.

"When they disowned me, I didn't just take this key. I took another set. To my parents' car. I used it to drive all the way out of Oklahoma and ended up in Hamilton. I spent two years there as an eventual wheelman for this guy, Kane, and his crew. But they found me."

I lay my hand over hers, covering my brand. "My parents, I mean. They said Donovan wanted me to repent and return to the fold. That Emily already gave birth to a son, but she was now pregnant with his daughter. The prophet finally realized how important it was to strengthen the congregation... that, if I confessed my sins and vowed to follow his word again, I could marry his daughter when she was grown."

Kylie sucks in a breath. "No, he fucking didn't."

I nod into the dark. "I remember saying something like, so I wait twenty-one more years to make my ex's kid my wife? And my mother... my *mother*... patted my arm and said, if I'm faithful again to the church, it would only be about fifteen. That the prophet *promised*."

I was twenty-five at the time. They were telling me that, at forty-one, I'd finally get a chance to fuck—and it would be Emily's fifteen-year-old daughter.

Luckily, Kylie comes to the same conclusion as I did then: "Your mother sucks."

"I know. And while they waited for me, expecting me to be their doting son and do what they said, I packed my shit, ducked out through the back, and took off. I hid out for a week, then shit went down in Hamilton... a job went bad... and I left. I didn't stop running until I hit Springfield and I discovered the West Side was ruled by a man called 'Devil'."

For the first time since I rolled onto my back, I turn to look at Kylie. "I figured the only way to get them to leave me alone was to show my allegiance to the devil for once and for all. The devil or just Devil, it didn't matter. And you know what? He saved me."

She ghosts her fingers over the height of my nearest cheek. "Nah."

223

"Nah?"

"Don't give that murderer all the credit, ace. From the way I see it, you saved yourself." She pats that cheek. "Now, let's go have some lunch."

I nod, even as I can't help but think: Save myself? Maybe.

But I won't stop until I save *her*.

I'M ACTUALLY PRETTY GLAD THAT KYLIE KNOWS JUST HOW much I owe Devil Crewes. Between that and how close we've gotten in the last two weeks, trapped together in Burns's cabin, I think I accomplished what I set out to.

The morning after Christmas, she announced that —if only for my sake—she wouldn't tell anyone about what she saw. That, if it was important to me that Devil get away with murder, then she was okay with it, too.

Part of me wondered if she only told me so because she thought it was what I needed to hear to finally drive her back to Springfield. Only I know now that she doesn't even live there. She doesn't live anywhere. Not really. She travels for work, taking shots every-where she goes, living in and out of hotels. She shies away from the topic whenever I bring it up, but I assume she's some big-time photographer.

Too bad I don't know her last name. There's count-less Kylie's with photo credits when I look them up, and even when I add an 'H' as a surname—assuming that that's what the tat on her hand stands for—I can't narrow it down.

And I need to.

I need to know everything about her.

In a very short time, this girl has become my life. My world. She's what I think about first thing in the morning, waking up wrapped around her. Her smile. Her laugh. Her humor.

Her *taste*.

She owns my thoughts. My fantasies. I'm fucking obsessed, and if she didn't return my affection, I'd use every ounce of my upbringing to push her away. To remind myself that I'm not worthy of such an angel on earth.

But she does care. Oh, I know there's no way she feels a sliver of the emotions I have for her. How can she? We just met... but it seems like I've waited twenty-seven years for her. So maybe ours isn't a first meeting to brag about, especially when you consider that I've been her sole companion and undeniable captor these last two weeks. It doesn't matter. I've waited my whole life for a woman like Kylie. Now that I have, I don't want to lose her.

But she finally agreed. I got what I wanted from her. Sure, I want *more*, but if she's going to keep Sinners Syndicate secrets... there's no reason for me to keep her as a captive any longer. Only it doesn't seem as if either of us are in a rush to leave just yet.

There's one good thing about it being directly after

Christmas. I don't expect to hear anything from Devil, Springfield, or the rest of the outside world. It was quiet in the lead-up to Christmas. I'm sure it'll be the same before New Year's.

And I get to believe that for two more days before I get a phone call.

From the beginning of our stay at the cabin, I kept expecting Kylie to go after my phone. I didn't get one until I was long gone from Donovan, starting over in Hamilton instead. Though she's only a year younger than me, she's basically grown up always having access to her own phone. I figured that was the hardest part of being my captive, but Kylie never seemed to care.

Burns doesn't have a landline or a computer in the cabin, even if he does have internet access. Without my phone, we'd be completely cut off from the outside world. Surprisingly, she thinks that's the fun part of being up here with me.

Fun. That's what she called it. *Fun.*

She's gotten used to my fellow Sinners—and Burns, though I'm careful not to let her know it's a cop who owns this cabin—checking in with me through the phone. Whenever it rings, she either heads into the basement to give me privacy or, more recently, tells me to take the call outside while she finishes watching whatever we have on the TV.

I don't even wait for her impatient shooing motion. Once the phone rings and I see **BOSS** in big, bold letters on the screen, I point to the door. She nods, and I slip outside.

The entire time she's been here with me, she's never tried to escape. She could have easily, but she doesn't, and I don't even think twice about heading outside to take this call.

Once the door is closed behind me, I answer. "Hello?"

"Kid. It's me."

"Hey, boss. What's up?"

The Devil of Springfield has earned his reputation. He's a gruff, tough son of a bitch, but if you're loyal to him, he can be your best friend. He called me on Christmas, despite knowing I don't actually celebrate the holiday, and he's been checking in on the situation as much as he has Rolls calling me.

That's why I expect at least a cursory question about how the girl and I spent the rest of the holiday. But I don't get it. Instead, Devil launches right into the conversation with a very pointed statement:

"The Hummingbird is working for Johnny Winter."

It takes me a second to make sense of what he said. The Hummingbird... "Cross told me about him. The mysterious hired hitman who burned down Cross's studio. Shit. Is that why he was targeted? Because Winter ordered the hit?" My stomach goes tight. "He's got reasons to be pissed at me. Is that why you're calling? Am I next?"

Devil's answer is a soft growl. "Not quite, Luca.

And, far as we can tell, Winter didn't order the hit on Cross. Someone else did, using the same assassin. But Winter made the most recent contract." The boss's voice develops a harsher edge. "On *me*."

What?

"Do you need me back? You don't have to worry about the girl anymore... Devil? I can help."

"Fuck, yeah, I need you back, but not for the reason you're thinking."

"Boss?"

"Listen to me, Luca. The contract community isn't as big as you'd guess with all the fucking mafia guys and crooks coming after us. You know of the Reed twins?"

I've heard of them. A pair of deranged identical twins who Devil hires out as killers whenever he wants a hit, but he doesn't want it falling back on him. One of them is the brains of the operation. The other is the muscle. "In Shadowvale, right?"

"You got it. Once it got out that the Hummingbird would be coming after me, Nicholas Reed"—the brains—"took it upon himself to figure out who the Hummingbird is, especially since she seems to have disappeared since taking the contract. She's supposed to be good, too, but she ain't as good as she thinks. Too many of her clients saw her damn face."

Hang on—

"*She*?"

thou shall not...

EIGHTEEN
HUMMINGBIRD

LUCA

"That's right," Devil says. "It's a woman. Mid-twenties. Brown skin. Brown hair. Curly. Brown eyes. Sound familiar? She has another distinguishing feature, too: a small 'H' tattoo on her hand that stands for Hummingbird."

No. *No.* "Devil..."

"I know. Soon as Reed filled me in, I knew exactly who he was talking about."

No. "Kylie? He thinks it's Kylie?"

"Could be. Description checks out, though I don't know about any Kylie. Her name changes all the time, but her MO never does. She leaves a hummingbird at every scene."

I know. Cross had one.

But if she was supposed to kill *Devil*?

"Was there one outside of Blockbuster?" I ask. I mean, if that's why she was there, and we caught her, wouldn't she have dropped one behind before we got her in the trunk?

"Royce and his crew went back and checked. Nothing there."

"She didn't have one on her, either. You checked her pockets that night. No hummingbird figure."

So she has similar features, down to the 'H'. So the Hummingbird has seemed to disappeared once we locked Kylie away in the mountain cabin. It can't be—

"I know. But what about you? Did you check the car?"

"I... no. When I pulled her out of the trunk, I didn't think to search under the trash liners I left in there." I was too focused on getting her inside of the cabin. After that, it just never occurred to me. But now... the skin. The curls. The 'H'...

'H' for Hummingbird.

"Hang on, boss. I'm going to check right now."

Keeping my phone to my ear, I grab the car keys that I keep habitually in whatever pants I'm wearing. Popping the trunk, I quickly run my gaze over the bags. Nothing stands out against the black plastic. Shoving them aside, I look at the interior beneath it.

Nothing.

"No." I start to lift the flap that covers the spare tire. "There's nothing—*fuck*."

"You find something, kid?"

I did. Nestled on top of the spare, I found *two* somethings.

"A bird figurine," I tell him. And it looks just like the one Cross showed me a couple of weeks ago. It's blue instead of that motley mix of purples and pinks, but I know what this is. "In the seam of the trunk, I found a hummingbird."

And a knife.

Before I drugged her and tipped her into the trunk, she was carrying a hummingbird figurine and a knife. Somehow, she hid them with the spare so we wouldn't find them on her, but they couldn't belong to anyone else but Kylie.

But the Hummingbird.

Fuck.

I'M NOT A GOOD LIAR.

The only way I was able to trick Winter was by telling him the damn truth. I went in as Luca St. James. I wasn't lying when I said I had history in Hamilton, and though it had been three years since I left Kane's crew, it didn't take much asking around to verify my story.

If I'd been there for more than the couple of days it took to break Cross and Genevieve out, Winter would've realized something was off. Luckily, that didn't happen. We made it out, and no one had heard anything about the leader of the Snowflakes... until one of the Dragonflies caught on to the fact that Vice Mayor Collins was working with Winter and told Damien Libellula.

Devil took Collins out as soon as he heard that the vice mayor was working with one of our enemies. These last two weeks, I believed it was one big coincidence that Kylie was on Skid Row when we were.

Now, I know that it wasn't a coincidence. Or maybe it was. I don't fucking know. She could've gotten lucky, or she might've been following the town car, trying to get close to Devil.

Because he was the assassin's target.

Because Johnny Winter hired *Kylie* to kill him.

If I was a good liar, I'd figure out a way to trick her into revealing her alter ego. If I didn't give a shit about my captive, her deception wouldn't hurt so damn bad.

But I'm not, and I do, and before I can even think about what I'm going to do about this, I leave the knife in the trunk, out of her reach, fist the hummingbird figurine, and march into the cabin.

"You're a hitman," I burst out, startling enough that she rises up from the couch as I slam the door shut behind me. "A hired hitman. A fucking contract killer, Kylie." I show her the figurine I found in the car. "Lose something... Hummingbird?"

She barely even hesitates before she juts her chin up at me.

"I didn't lose it. I knew exactly where I put it. Trunk,

right?" Walking toward me without a care in the world, she holds out her palm. Wordlessly, I drop the bluish figurine into her waiting hand. "And I prefer the term hitwoman. Girls can be homicidal killers, too, you know."

My mouth falls open. "You're not going to deny it?"

"What's the point? The way you came storming in here like that? You obviously know. I like you, ace. I'm not going to insult your intelligence by denying it just so you can call me a liar. I'm tired of having to hide who I am from you." She pouts. "It wasn't fun anymore."

"So you are a hitman—"

"Hitwoman, and yes. I was. Until some mafia driver got between me and my target."

Devil.

"So that's true, too? The contract you took... you were hired to kill Devil? My boss?"

"I wanted a high-profile hit," she says, as though that excuses it. "The last time I was in Springfield, the target survived."

Target...

Cross.

"You tried to kill my friend," I grit out through clenched teeth.

"Relax, Luca. It wasn't personal."

Wasn't personal? If Cross hadn't escaped the fire, we would've found him among the ashes. "Thou shall not kill."

She snorts, and while it seemed like she was trying to keep me calm a moment ago, now her brown eyes darken in sudden annoyance. "You spout that shit at Devil? 'Cause, last time I checked, he murders people. A lot of people. In fact, your boss offing a guy is the reason we got together, ace."

Wait—

I stumble back on my heels. I know it shouldn't matter at this moment, but... "We're together?"

Kylie glares up at me. "You think I let just anyone fuck my ass? You were only the second—"

No, no.

No.

I surge forward, cupping her face in my hands. "You're pissed. I'm pissed, too. I never... I never expected this. But if you care about me at all, don't talk about other guys. Not in front of me. Please." I'm pleading. How did this happen? One second, I was furious that she lied to me. And now... "*Please*."

She jerks her head out of my hold, loose curls snagging on my fingers. "Why do you care anyway?"

Why do I care?

"Because you're mine, Kylie."

And I'm tired of pretending otherwise.

Huh. Maybe I am a better liar than I thought, too, if she didn't know that...

"Kylie? I'm the Hummingbird, remember? Just another killer you look down your nose on. Don't pretend like that's not a dealbreaker for you, Luca."

It should be. "Kylie... I just. Look. I'm all fucked-up right now. Devil called and told me that one of our contacts learned about the hit on his head. They knew it was the Hummingbird's contract. Of course Reed's gonna do what he can to figure out who you are. We have a good relationship with Shadowvale. He doesn't want to see Devil dead. None of us do. But you... you're a killer?"

That's what I'm stuck on. More than the lies and the deception, it's how easily I was fooled because she's, well, *Kylie*.

And I should know better. Savannah Libellula is a tiny thing with almost more leaves decorating her bicep than any other Dragonfly enforcer. I got a front-row seat to what she's capable of when she pretended to be Falco's girlfriend in order to end up in Winter's cells.

She's a killer, and I never judged her for that. So why am I being a hypocrite and judging *this* woman?

Because I love her, I realize. Because I'm obsessed with her. Because she owns my thoughts... my fantasies... *all* of me.

But if I fell for who she was pretending to be instead of the real Kylie Ferguson, I don't really love *her* at all, do I?

I lost Emily once. I thought my life was over. Losing Kylie now?

I—

"I am. I am a killer," Kylie tells me flatly. "You want

to know how I got into the job? Because I killed Jason Villa, my sister's first husband. She was twenty-one when she got married, just like you wanted to do. I was sixteen when I realized that wedding vows don't mean shit. To honor and obey? In sickness and in health? That fucker put my sister in the hospital three times in the six weeks they were married. He was the hazard to her health. So I shot him."

Is that it? "You were defending someone you love—"

She scoffs. "Don't make me seem like a hero. I killed that prick. I liked it, too. It was *fun*. So I did it again. And again. Eventually, I realized I could get paid for it. And you're right. About a month ago, I accepted a hit on Lincoln Crewes. I heard he would be at the Blockbuster that night, and that was why I was there. To kill him. And now I'm here. And I thought we hit it off, but... *shit*. I don't know what's going to happen next, but—"

I don't care.

Maybe I'm not as big a hypocrite as I thought. Because while I understand why she chose the life she did—becoming a murderess as a teen—that also influenced the woman she became. The woman I've gotten to know.

The woman I need.

And it hits me. I... I don't care that she's the Hummingbird. That she lied. Wouldn't I have done the same thing?

Didn't I do the same thing when I returned to Hamilton to work for Johnny Winter, knowing I was doing it all to rescue Cross and Genevieve on Devil's order?

All along, I've been following the Devil of Springfield. I measured my morals by the archaic commandments that I've clung to like a lifeline. As long as I don't break all ten, I'm a good guy.

Fuck that. I'm a Sinner.

As a Sinner, there are rules I have to live by.

As Luca, I have my own.

I'll break them all for her.

Because I'm also a Sinner who's been a disciple of Lincoln Crewes ever since I made a deal with Devil. I followed him, and being a part of the mafia life has led me to my very own Lilith.

Kylie Ferguson.

A temptation in the flesh created perfectly for Luca St. James, she could do absolutely anything—and I'd find a way to justify it.

Just like I do now.

"You didn't kill him."

She gives me a look of pure exasperation. It's *adorable*. "I was going to. I heard what he did to that homeless guy fifteen years ago. How he got his nickname. *Devil*. I was even gonna hack his head off when I was done."

Reaching out, grabbing my girl, I squeeze Kylie to me. "Please, for the love of everything that's fucking holy, never repeat that again."

"Don't worry, ace. That was when Winter was paying me to get Devil. I'm on Devil's side now. Or I will be if he gives me a chance to explain."

I pull back, my heart suddenly pounding. "You are? You're loyal to the Sinners now?"

In our line of work, loyalty counts for a lot. And, well, she didn't kill the boss.

That should count for *something*, right?

She shrugs, then leans in, snuggling as close to me as possible. "Well, I'm on your side, so I guess I'll root for the Sinners, too. But I have unfinished business with Johnny Winter. He paid me half up front for a dead Devil. I missed my deadline, but I pride myself on completing every job. Well, except for one. Your friend, I guess. That fire on the West Side, but the target didn't die, and then my client disappeared afterward—"

"Mickey Kelly," I supply. "He threatened Cross's girl. Said he was going to go after Genevieve next, and Cross... he didn't like that idea."

Considering Cross beat him to death with his bare hands, that's putting it mildly.

"Well, he didn't hire me for that hit, I'll tell you that much. Winter, either. Right now, it's just Lincoln Crewes I was supposed to take out. It's why I had the strychnine on me along with the knife and my hummingbird figurine. If I couldn't get him down on my own, that would have done the trick."

"Strychnine?" I ask. It sounds familiar, but fuck if I know what that is.

Kylie nods. "The lip gloss that's in my jacket pocket. It's really a poison solution in case I get in trouble."

I blink. Devil looked her over. Besides the cash, all she had was a tube of lip gloss.

"That was *poison*?"

"It is."

Is... because she has it stowed in the pocket of the jacket tossed on the floor in the basement. "Wait. Are you telling me that you could've poisoned me at any point?"

"Apart from all the other ways an experienced hitwoman like me could kill a sweetheart like you? Oh, yeah. I mean, just so you don't feel left out, I *was* gonna use it on you once I got bored of you. To get you back for drugging me."

Holy shit.

I can't believe I ever felt worried for Kylie. If anyone was ever in danger here, it's been *me*.

Same thing with my worry that she was pretending to be someone else to hide that she was also the Hummingbird. No way. She's still Kylie, just with a killer secret.

And, fuck, I think I know why I was so riled up. Not because I want to be all-holier-than-thou. Nope. It's because it's fucking hot as hell that my girl is an assassin.

Especially when she pats my chest in that way she

has before telling me, "You're lucky I decided I like you, ace."

Is that what she thinks?

Even knowing that her lip gloss is fucking *poison,* that doesn't stop me from dropping my head low, finding her mouth with mine. Mimicking fucking with my tongue, I take her mouth until she's gasping for breath while I'm still holding her to me tightly.

Only then do I collar the back of her neck, tilting her head up so that she's forced to meet the look in my eye as I tell her, "No. I'm a lucky fucking bastard because you *love* me."

She smirks at me. "Who says I love you?"

I grin at my girl. "You did."

"Oh?"

I nip her slightly swollen lip. "When you didn't poison me."

"Keep pushing your luck. I could change my mind."

"I thought you had unfinished business with Winter," I remind her.

"Oh, I do. I'm going to kill him. I've got a plan, too. And if we can figure out a way to keep Devil from coming after me first, I think he might not be too pissed off that I'm the Hummingbird. Not when I'm more than ready to swap sides."

I really fucking hope so.

thou shall not...

NINETEEN
THE PLAN

LUCA

t takes me nearly an hour to convince Devil to hear her out, to explain that the Hummingbird is willing to swap sides and help us end Johnny Winter for once and for all, but I was determined.

Turns out, I was also way wrong. The boss doesn't want me to kill her myself now that we know she's the Hummingbird. He wants me to find a way to get her in the car—backseat, front, trunk… he wasn't particular— and drive her back to Springfield. There, he would take his time learning everything he could about the mysterious hitman—sorry, hit*woman*—who had been flitting around the States, killing without anyone but her clients knowing she was doing so.

Just like how he made the vice mayor talk, he'd get Kylie to spill her guts. He might even use his knife to spill her *actual* guts. I already was sure that I couldn't let that happen, but unless I wanted to spend the rest of my life knowing that Devil was gunning for me, I needed to find a way to do what I was told while also protecting Kylie.

It made it easier for me that she decided she would talk, none of Devil's specialized persuasion necessary. Before I got back on the phone with Devil, I had names, dates, numbers, and all the intel that would hold him over before he lost his temper completely and drove up to the mountains himself.

More than that, I had Kylie's plan on how to take down Winter. Just like how Winter thought that, cutting off Devil's head would be the end of the Sinners Syndicate, if the second Winter twin is dead, the Snowflakes will scatter. We can keep them out of our turf, and maybe even start gathering up their operation and rolling it into ours.

It took an hour, but by the time I was done, Devil gave me his word that he wouldn't shoot her on sight. Her plan had enough merit to intrigue him. If she could serve us Winter's head on a silver platter instead of going for the boss's, he might even look past the fact she accepted a contract on his life.

Might being the operative word there, but I fucking clung to it the entire ride back to the city.

I forgave Kylie. That's all she wanted. She sat in the front seat, commenting on the mountain terrain and scenery all the way up until we returned to civilization.

She seemed sure that Devil would accept her switching sides, though even she stumbled a step or two when I walked her into the meeting room in the back of the Devil's Playground only for her to see eight unfriendly faces staring back at her.

I knew to expect Devil there. Royce is his second so obviously he's involved. Tanner's our tech genius. Damien Libellula came since the Snowflakes infiltrating Springfield affected him as much as anyone here; same for his wife, who has become one of the Dragonflies' top enforcers since hooking up with the older man. Devil insisted on Officer Burns being here for the meet. Burns brought along his rookie partner, Officer Coleman for some reason.

And Cross is here, too.

A lump lodges in my throat. Cross... the very Sinner who lost his livelihood—and almost his life—when the Hummingbird burned down his studio.

When *Kylie* burned down his studio...

I can't bring myself to look at Cross just yet. Instead, I nod at Burns, a silent 'thank you' for letting us borrow the cabin, then come to a stop before Devil, clutching Kylie's hand.

His dark eyes look her over. "Yup. That's the girl who was there at Blockbusters," he confirms.

Rolls raises his eyebrows. "*This* is the Hummingbird?"

Pacing behind Rolls, Cross huffs.

I squeeze Kylie's hand. Or maybe she squeezes

mine. I can't tell, though I do run my thumb over the faded 'H' on her skin.

She grins at the group assembled. "Okay. Hi. I can sense the tension in the air. Get the feeling none of you like me and, hey, I get it. Wouldn't like me, either, if I didn't know how fucking awesome I am."

Cross huffs louder.

Rolls gives him a warning look.

The rookie cop whispers something to Burns.

Kylie ignores it all.

"Okay. I've heard stories about the Devil of Springfield's infamous temper and just how short it is. Luca's too much of a sweetheart to tell me that there's a good chance I'm not walking out of this room alive. I get it. I understand it. So let's not waste any time. Yes, I am the Hummingbird. Yes, I was hired to burn down Sinners and Saints tattoo studio and kill Carlos 'Cross' da Silva. Yes, I obviously failed, but my track record speaks for itself. He's the only one who's survived the Hummingbird, so when I tell you that I can get Johnny Winter, I fucking mean it."

Like Devil, Libellula is wearing a suit. Unlike the head of the Sinners Syndicate, the other man's suit is impeccably tailored to, well, suit him. Devil looks like a big brawler poured into his, muscles bulging against the tight fabric. Libellula—with his silver-streaked hair and piercing blue eyes—seems like Hollywood's idea of a gangster.

Until he speaks in his no-nonsense, slightly

accented voice, and you wouldn't mistake him for anything other than the threat that he is.

"And how exactly do you plan on doing that? Enlighten us, if you would."

"Simple. By killing Lincoln Crewes first."

Okay. I know Kylie's plan. She ran through the outline of it for me before I brought it to Devil in the first place. I guess I just thought that the boss would've at least filled the others in before we met them at Sinners HQ.

From the reaction she gets, I'm thinking he might have forgotten to mention that part.

Rolls has his Beretta out, aimed right at Kylie. Savannah's stiletto knife appears in her hand as if by magic; considering I got to know her well enough when we were both undercover in Hamilton, helping to save Genevieve and Cross, I'm not surprised, though I'm no less impressed than I was the first time I saw her handle a blade. Libellula has his own gun out. So does Officer Burns.

And Cross. He's pulled a weapon on Kylie, and of everyone gathered, he looks the most ready to pull the trigger.

I know better than to believe he wouldn't. Maybe before I saw what captivity had done to him, I might've. But then I spoke to one of the other guards— Noah, the one that Genevieve was forced to shoot and kill—and he told me how Cross bit a guy's cock right off.

At the time, I couldn't help but think: it's always the quiet ones you have to look out for. I mean, I get why he did it. If someone put me on my knees and told me I had to suck dick, I might bite down, too. But hard enough to sever the tip?

He's dangerous. All of us Sinners are, but he has the most reason to want to see the Hummingbird grounded after Devil.

I don't even think. Letting go of her hand, I step in front of her.

If my brother is going to shoot the woman I need more than my next breath, he'll have to go through me first.

Cross swallows roughly.

Devil crosses his arms over his chest, watching the whole scene closely.

Kylie clicks her tongue. "Oh, for fuck's sake. Drop the weapons. I wasn't being literal."

Devil tilts his head in her direction. "So you're not going to kill me."

"No, and I know you already know that because Luca told you. But since the rest of your squad here is obviously out of the loop, let me rephrase that. I'm going to let everyone *think* I killed you."

"Think that's a smart idea?" calls out Burns. "The city's been on high alert since the vice mayor's body was found downtown, covered in bullet wounds and signs of torture."

"Fucker deserved it," mutters Devil.

"He was allowing the Snowflakes to sell their dirty Eclipse on my territory," cuts in Libellula. "I kept seeing their mark, but I couldn't understand it. Collins was their mule. I'm with Lincoln. He deserved worse."

"I get that, but that's not what I'm saying. Sarge has us roaming the streets in pairs. It's been like that all holiday season. Christmas might be done, and we all know Harrison doesn't give a fuck, but the department can sense trouble brewing."

His partner nods his head in agreement. "Even those of us not on the take... with New Year's coming, we're expecting something to pop off."

"That's my point," Kylie says. "It will. At least if someone here can get their hands on some explosives before the thirty-first."

Rolls gives her a speculative look. "I can get anything."

"A bomb?" Savannah twirls the stiletto. "That's your plan?"

"Part of it, yeah. See, Winter wants a spectacle. I say we give him a spectacle."

The plan is deceptively simple. With Devil's permission, I allowed Kylie to use my phone. She downloaded an app to give her a burner number, then reached out to Winer. After apologizing for missing her deadline, she point-blank offered to go after Devil again and make it explosive.

He grabbed onto the word. He promised to meet

her in person after, paying her a fraction of her fee if she did exactly that. Make it explosive.

"He wants me to blow up the Devil's Playground with Devil in it," she admits to the surprise of everyone —except for Devil and Tanner.

Probably because Devil *did* know, and Tanner is a genius who either figured it out already or figured there was a reason he was involved in this discussion. Oh, like using his brains to pull of an explosion...

"Blow up?" echoes Rolls. "No fucking way. Link, you can't—"

Kylie holds up both of her hands. Not only is she making it obvious that, unlike everyone else in the room, she isn't armed, but she catches Rolls's attention. "No. I talked him down from that. I know it's the Sinners' HQ, and I'm a hitwoman, but that's too much collateral damage, even for me. We settled on something a little more targeted. One of the offices off the back as long as I get video proof that Devil was in there when the bomb goes off. You said you can get me something that'll do it, right?"

Rolls is the best fixer we have. He wasn't bluffing. He really can get anything. "Yeah. I'm sure I can."

"Good. I have until New Year's to get it done." She turns toward the pair of beat cops in their uniform. "That's where you two come in. You'll take the call. Report that Devil was a casualty. I'll go and meet with Winter in person to let him know it's done. We always do that." Kylie rolls her eyes. "It's a power play for him.

And when I have him in my sights, I'll take him down." She waggles her fingers. "Bye-bye, Snowflakes."

Devil heard the plan earlier. He agreed to let Kylie lay it out in front of the people who would help us with her plan before making any other decisions.

I look at them all, trying to get a gauge of what they're thinking.

As I do, Kylie reminds them all why we're here. "He hired the Hummingbird to take down the head of the Sinners Syndicate." A nudge to my side, and then, "What's that saying, ace? An eye for an eye?"

I nod. "That's right."

"He wanted Devil," she says flatly. "To be honest, his plan was to go after Damien Libellula next—"

Savannah's features sharpen as she sucks in a breath. "Over my dead body."

Libellula strokes the length of her dark hair. "Cara mia," he murmurs softly.

"Just telling you that Winter... he won't be deterred from this. Who knows? He might even have hunted up another contractor to get it done while I was... you know... off the grid. It might not be the best shot, but I might be your *only* shot at getting to him."

"How can we trust you?" asks Cross. He stopped pacing, but unlike the others, he hasn't put away his gun yet, either. "You tried to kill me and didn't manage to do it. How do we know you'll really turn on your employer like this?"

Kylie snorts. "Don't flatter yourself. I did what I did

for money, and gave up when it was clear I wouldn't get pair for finishing it. It was just another job to me. But this—"

"Is your way of saving your skin?"

"Cross," I begin.

Kylie shakes her head royally. "Of course. But, more importantly, this kill would be a favor for someone I care about. I don't give a shit what *you* think. There's only one man in this room I want to prove myself to. And if Luca thinks I can do this, then I can."

Suddenly, all eyes are on me.

I lay my hand on her shoulder while meeting Devil's in particular. "I trust her," I say simply.

"Really?" snaps Cross. "A hired killer you just met?"

"I'll be retired once this is done," Kylie chimes in helpfully.

Wait.

What?

I look down at her, feeling myself falling for her impish grin all over again. "You are?"

She shrugs. "I've been thinking about it for a while. I like the idea of going out with a bang. When this is all done, the Hummingbird is going to retire."

"You don't have to do that because of me."

"I know. Killing was fun for a while, but I was getting bored. You know me, ace. I don't like to be bored. Luckily, I found someone who entertains me." She taps my bicep. "I get a kick out of corrupting you.

But don't worry. If you need me, I'll be there. One of us can be a killer from time to time."

And it doesn't have to be me.

Thou shall not—

"Come on." Cross shakes his head. "This is ridiculous. We know Winter's still sneaking around Springfield. For the first time in months, we know he's near. I think we should take her out, then handle Winter and the Snowflakes on our own." His voice drops, almost deadly quiet. "He tried to hurt Genevieve. I can't let him go after her again."

If Winter's dead, Cross won't have to worry about that.

Too bad the overprotective, possessive artist isn't thinking rationally. He's thinking about his butterfly, and how far he'll go to protect her.

How do I know? Because the moment Cross lifts his gun again, aiming it at Kylie, I draw *mine*.

Have I ever aimed my Ruger at another person? No. But if he thinks that he's going to shoot this woman in front of me?

We can *both* be killers.

Cross narrows his gaze on the barrel of my gun. "This how you gonna get your next slash, Luca?"

Luca, I notice. Not 'wheels' anymore.

I guess that makes sense. I do have a gun on him.

My hand is steady, the gun focused on Cross's chest. "If you threaten Kylie again, it might be."

"Drop the gun, Luca," rumbles Devil. "Don't make a stupid choice, kid. He's one of us."

"So was Twig," I remind the boss, "but you didn't hesitate to put him down when he disrespected Ava."

"She's my wife. My fucking heart. I love her. Of course I did."

"And I'll do the same."

Rolls mutters a curse under his breath. Officer Coleman inches a couple of steps away from Cross.

He's not even looking at the gun. No. His gaze is on my face. "You love her, Luca?"

That's too mild of a word for how I feel about Kylie Ferguson. I'm *obsessed* with her.

I know it's fast. I know we only just met. I know she's a contract killer who lied to me about who she really was.

And, like I said, I don't give a fuck about that. Because she's Kylie, and she's *mine*.

But how can I say all that? With a room full of people, and half of them looking like they're ready to turn their weapons on me now?

I drop the Ruger. "Yeah. I love her."

Cross nods. His eyes are still dark with rage, but his voice calms as he says, "Then I guess that's good enough for me. Come on. Let's blow up that sick motherfucker before he can hurt any more of us."

And that's how my future with Kylie Ferguson hinges on faking one death and pulling off another.

No fucking pressure.

TWENTY
PICK YOUR POISON

KYLIE

When the countdown on New Year's Eve hits zero all over the world, balls drop, fireworks go off, and couples kiss to mark the new year coming.

In Springfield, I thought it was poetic to set off the C4 detonator at the exact moment the clock struck midnight.

Everything was planned to the last detail. Up until the moment that Devil himself pressed the button that made everything go *boom*, I was working with Tanner to make my plan work. As the mafia fixer, Rolls McIntyre got what we needed to build the explosive. Of course, it was my twisted brain that came up with the plan. Tanner built the bomb and, using his computer know-how, helped me create a video to send to Winter so that he knows I'm working on taking Lincoln Crewes out.

After being 'missing' for weeks, I wanted to show Winter that I was all about finishing my contract. Smart as he is, he should've realized something was up when I offered to create the spectacle at a discount. I think, at this point, he was just so eager to take over Springfield for once and for all that he would've believed anything if it meant that Devil was out of his way.

I don't know why he targeted Devil. If Damien and his assassin wife—who I'm very interested in getting to know once this is all taken care of—were responsible for Jimmy Winter's death, it would've made sense that he'd go after the Dragonflies first, especially when he was interested in both the drug and counterfeiting trade ruled by the Libellula Family. The only thing I can think is that it was Devil who embarrassed *Johnny*.

And not even the man himself. It was his Sinners.

Cross da Silva was taken by Winter and his men mainly because he was part of Devil's inner circle. More importantly, though, he had a thing going with Genevieve Libellula even before they were held captive together. Getting to Damien by going through his baby sister was a stroke of genius—until Luca slipped in under Winter's nose, helping facilitate the break-out.

It was Devil and his men who humiliated Johnny Winter. And it was Devil who needed to die.

Well, not really. He did sacrifice two rooms off the

back of the large building that houses the Devil's Playground, as well as the rest of the Sinners' head-quarters. While I worked with Rolls and Tanner, Luca and some of the other Sinners in the know snuck in through the back to remove anything essential before it blew. They packed the rooms surrounding it with insulation in a bid to eliminate any further damage and blocked off the area out back, claiming they needed the space for a New Year's Eve event.

At eleven-forty-four, Devil entered the back. On his arm, Savannah Libellula, wearing a coat with a hood that hid her face. I snapped pictures as they slipped in so that I would have the timestamp, hoping to pass them off as Mr. and Mrs. Crewes arriving at the Sinners HQ just before midnight.

The real Mrs. Crewes, along with the Crewses's young daughter, was under heavy protection at their penthouse apartment. With Rolls on-site at the Play-ground, making sure nothing goes wrong, he made sure his own wife was waiting with Devil's. Though my plan hinged on making it seem as if he was out for the night, celebrating with the missus, there was pure murder on his face when I suggested it. Message received. No way in hell was he letting the Humming-bird near his wife, and thankfully Damien's offered to play the part.

Everything went off without a hitch. At midnight, Devil exploded his own empty offices, and I was watching from a distance to get proof. The rumor mill was working over time, both gangs banding together to spread the word that there were two casualties: Lincoln and Ava Crewes. In reality, Savannah went home with Damien, Luca drove Devil back home to his wife, and I sat under Rolls's scrutinizing gaze while I waited for him to return for me.

When it comes to babysitters, I definitely prefer Luca.

Officer Burns and Coleman handled the police report. The news picked it up, too, which only furthered my proof that I had accomplished what I set out to do: take down the Devil of Springfield. Devil murmured the name 'Lazarus' when he realized that, in a couple of days, he'll have to either stay under or let the rest of the city he rules know he's alive.

That, coupled with the rosary tatted on his arm, made me finally understand why a man with as much religious trauma as Luca has so willingly followed one christened 'Devil'...

For now, though, he's 'dead'. It's been two days since I 'killed' him, and I'm finally going to meet Johnny Winter to settle my contract.

At least, that's what the dark-haired, dark-suited man in the corner of the coffeehouse thinks is going to happen. Me? Fucking plans. I'm full of them.

And it's up to me to pull this one off on my own.

It had to happen this way. Luca tried to insist that

he join me, but for the last two years, I made my rep on working alone. Winter would know something was up right away if I brought him with me, and I couldn't even let him chauffeur me across state lines because I always rent a car and drive myself if I can.

Plus, we both agreed that I'd disappear for a couple of days if I managed to pull this off. That's also pretty common for me, and especially now that I know Nicholas and Hunter Reed have figured out my identity, it's probably for the best that I lie low before figuring out my next move... and I'm not fooling even myself because I already have a plan.

I usually do.

Today's involved arriving at the coffeehouse, scoping out the car most likely to belong to Winter, slapping the C4 explosive to the underside, then meeting up with the man himself. I would pass over the thumb drive with all the proof I had that I finished off Devil Crewes, verify that I picked the right car, wait for him to drive off, and when I blew *him* up, that would be another round of poetic justice.

You know what the best thing about plans are? That they're never set in stone.

When I arrive at the coffeehouse, I don't check the parking lot. I head right in, glancing around the space. I pick out two buff guys on different sides of the crowded shop. One is wearing a football jersey and jeans. The other is more stylishly dressed, clad in a turtleneck and khakis. Each one has a perfect vantage point toward the door, plus the man sitting in front of an expensive laptop in the corner.

Johnny Winter and two of his goons, I'm betting.

Pretending that I didn't see them, I bop along, listening to the nonexistent music in my headphones. Only pulling them off, resting them around the back of my neck when the barista takes my order, I pay for my coffees and move toward the side counter to wait for them.

Out of the corner of my eye, Winter is watching me. I turn, giving him a quick wave before paying attention for the barista to call out the fake name I offered her.

I ordered the coffees black. Accepting them from the girl at the counter, I mosied over to the spot where customers can doctor their own drinks. I do, leaving one alone while pouring a splash of cream and three Sweet 'n Lows into the other. A quick touch-up with my lip gloss, and with a cheery smile tugging on my lips, I carry both of the coffees over to Johnny Winter.

Tucking my bag onto my lap, I slide into the booth before placing both of the coffees on the tabletop.

"Sorry about the wait. I needed a hit of caffeine and, well, you did tell me to meet you at a coffee shop." I tap the lid on the left one. "This one's black, no milk, no sugar." I tap the right one. "This has some cream and two of those pink packets. Pick your poison."

Winter purses his lips. "I prefer the one with cream, if you're offering."

That kind of surprises me. "Wow. Would've taken

you for a black coffee drinker. Good thing I can drink every type of coffee. Here you go." I push the right cup toward him.

Winter lifts the cup. Not surprisingly, the suspicious bastard lifts up the lid. He takes a sniff, then nods. It's obviously the coffee with cream and sweetener, and after he replaces the lid, he takes a sip.

He waits expectantly.

I lift mine and swallow.

He drinks again, then lowers his cup. "Actually," he says after a moment, "I do prefer a strong cup of coffee without anything added to it. However, I saw you pour something into the black coffee, and I thought it would be rude to refuse the offer of a free beverage from one of my employees."

Because that's what I'm supposed to be, right? A hired hitwoman.

The thumb drive of 'evidence' is in my bag. We're not supposed to chat. I pass over the thumb drive, he checks the files on his computer, I get payment wired to my account.

Then again, I've never bought him coffee before.

I shrug. "Did I?"

"And, yet, you drink it."

He thinks I did.

I use my fingernail to tap the side of his paper cup. "Did you see me doctor up this one?"

"Yes. The cream, as you said. And the fake sugar packets. Three of them, though. Not two."

So he *was* watching.

Sitting up in my seat, I smile brightly at him. "Don't forget the strychnine."

Strychnine is odorless. He could sniff that coffee all he wants, and he'd never know I added anything other than what I said. The three Sweet 'n Lows were meant to try to hide the bitter taste of the poison if that's the cup he chose. I figured, if he went for the straight coffee, the bitter coffee itself could explain away the taste.

He took two sips. By my calculations, that should be enough.

Regular strychnine will show its effects in about fifteen to thirty minutes. Not everyone dies from a moderate dose, either. It won't be pleasant, but they can survive it.

Which is why the strychnine I keep in my lip gloss container is concentrated in a liquid form that will lead to death in less than a minute.

Does Winter know that? Maybe. I can see the sudden realization that he's been poisoned in his dark eyes, in the way he reaches up, clutching his throat, and how his face starts to turn red.

I take that as my cue to go.

Taking my untouched, poisoned cup of coffee that I faked drinking with me so that I don't inadvertently kill anyone else, I start scooting out of the booth.

His free hand clutches the table. His mouth opens, ready to shout for his two goons to stop me, maybe for them to help him, but that's when the choking starts.

I rise up from my seat.

Slapping the table now, Winter tries to push himself up.

Across the way, Football Jersey rises. I don't know where Turtleneck is, but here's hoping I can slip by him in the aftermath of what's about to happen.

Strolling away with my own cup, I start for the exit. At the same time, I hear a *thud* behind me. In the window's reflection, I see Football Jersey racing for his boss, and Johnny Winter seizing on the ground, still choking though the sudden din in the room as others realized that he's having a medical episode drowns it out.

Turtleneck appears, stepping out of the bathroom and walking into a disaster. His eyes find me. With my free hand, I shove my headphones up over my ears, bump the door with my ass, and walk out into the cold.

After that, I walk leisurely toward my rental with the certainty that the second goon will rush over to check on Johnny Winter rather than follow me. They think they know who I am. They'll think they can get help for their boss, then come after me.

But I'm the Hummingbird, and I don't plan on being caught again. Besides, I have a flight to catch.

As I start the car, pulling out of the lot as I didn't have a single care in the world, I listen for the inevitable blare of an ambulance as I think about what

I just did. Devil was meant to be a high-profile hit. In a way, it was. As far as Johnny Winter knows, the other mafia leader died in that explosion.

But he's going to choke to death on poison in the middle of a retail coffee house in Hamilton without any real fanfare at all.

Know what? Seems like a fitting end to me.

thou shall not...

TWENTY-ONE
MINE

KYLIE

In the middle of bumfuck Oklahoma, it was a million times easier to get my hands on an untraceable gun than it was to find anyone who would give me information on the Holy Church of Jesus Devotion.

Within three hours of landing at the OKC Airport, I had my choice between a scraped Ruger, a Colt, and a Smith & Wesson. As a nod to Luca, I went with the Ruger, then flirted with the hick selling me the weapon until I was sure he'd remember more about my tits and ass than my face if it ever came to him having to identify me.

And though Andy was more than willing to take sex in exchange for the Ruger—which I passed on, handing him five hundreds instead—he flinched, then played dumb when I asked about the church run by Jack Donovan.

From what Luca told me, it's a secluded cult that lives in a small community named after the prick who thinks he's their god. I know it's called Donovan, but it's not on any map. I couldn't find shit about it online using my burner phone. I would've thought Luca made the whole thing up, only I saw that brand on his arm, and I noticed the way Andy flinched.

It's real, and it takes me nearly all of the time I allotted in Oklahoma to find it.

Luckily for me, I find a lead in the last place I expect: a little old lady eating breakfast by herself at a Cracker Barrel. I stopped there to grab a bite on my way to see if a local Southern Baptist Church had any idea where to find Donovan. She seemed lonely, and fuck knows I can be an empathetic ear when I want to be, and we struck up a conversation over biscuits, eggs, and bacon.

Mary Su had heard of Donovan. Mary Su has a cousin's friend's daughter who married a man involved with that sacrilegious church. Mary Su didn't like how the priest called himself a prophet, or how he had three young children with that browbeaten wife of his, all while whoring around with some of the young ladies in Oklahoma City because *thou shall not commit adultery* is one of the commandments Jack Donovan has no problem flaunting.

Mary Su doesn't think a good girl like me should

have anything to do with those fake Christian heathens, but if I insist, she'll jot down the approximate location on this napkin for me.

Thank you, Mary Su.

From the outskirts, Donovan looks like a retirement community. Built on a large expanse of flat lands, there are multiple apartment buildings, all surrounded by a massive—and I mean *massive*—church in the center. Elaborate and expensive, it glitters like gold in the sunlight.

I figured I would find Jack Donovan and his altar in there. If not in the sanctuary, then a place where he could lord over the rest of his 'congruents'. I park the car I rented under another one of my fake IDs in the nearest lot to the church. There aren't many there. Despite it being the first week of January, and fucking *cold* out, there are people milling out everywhere you look, walking all over the place.

Just like always, if you walk with certainty, as if you belong where you are, no one will ever doubt that you do. So while I catch a few curious stares from the people outside, no one actually approaches me on my way to the church.

No one, that is, except for one man.

"Hello. I don't think I've seen your face around Donovan before. Can I help you?"

I have an immediate refusal halfway to my lips when I glance up at the man who's blocking my path. He's about mid-forties, sandy color hair dotted with a few grey strands. It's his eyes, though, that make me do a double-take.

I know those eyes.

This man is the spitting image of Luca, only about twenty years older.

Holy shit. I think this is his *dad*.

Can he help me?

I smile. "Yes, actually. I'm new in town. I'm interested in finding a church that lines up with my ideals. One of the local pastors recommended that I'd be a perfect fit for the Holy Church of Jesus Devotion. That I'd need to speak with Pastor Jack Donovan." I lower my voice, trying to adopt a tone of reverence when all I want to do is put my Ruger against Mr. St. James's gut and pull the trigger. "That the prophet might be interested in reforming a sinner like me."

Luca's father nods. On third glance, I notice that his eyes aren't exactly like his son's. There's the darkness of fanaticism lurking in their depths, and if he has any clue what I mean by my last comment—thank you for the tip, Mary Su—he doesn't care that his precious prophet is fucking bad girls on the side.

Instead, he seems quite eager to serve me up on a silver platter like some long-dead saint's head to his 'prophet'. I don't know what he was doing wandering by. Don't know where his wife is—and I have a thing or two I'd like to say to Luca's mother about the way she treated her son—but regardless of what he was in the middle of, he drops it to be my guide.

I'm not surprised that we head right for the church after all, though the pews being empty inside kind of strike me as a little weird. Who knows? Maybe, for all this being a 'holy' settlement built specifically for the Holy Church of who remembers that shit, the church is kept empty until the prophet wants to put on a show—

Hang on.

It's not *empty* empty. I mean, I don't see anyone at first glance, but two pretty peeved voices are coming from the doorway off the pulpit.

Mr. St. James hesitates. For a second, I'm sure he's going to steer me right back out so that I don't get the wrong idea about their cult. But, see, I already think anyone who willingly follows this fraud and maims their fucking son is trash so, ignoring the way he murmurs that the prophet is occupied, I just point toward the open doorway, then say cheerily, "He in there? I'm sure I can find him myself."

As if Luca's dad will allow that. I all but skip forward while he hurries at my heels, too stunned to do anything but follow me.

Halfway down the aisle, the voices quiet. I can sense the man's relief behind me, and I smirk.

Yeah. Remember how that feels while you can, buddy. Because, by the time I'm done, it'll be a distant memory—and I can't *wait*.

I pop my head into the office. Mr. St. James tiptoes

next to me before moving to stand a few steps in front of me.

There are two figures inside, and though their voices had dropped, it's obvious they were still having a quiet argument even as we walked in; three if you count the small baby that the woman is holding onto, chubby fists clutching her dress. The woman is about my age, a cascade of blonde hair moving with her as she swivels to see us entering the room before turning to look at the man behind the desk again.

I'll admit, the first thing that catches my eye after that is the twinkling cross the church leader has posted on the wall behind his desk, directly over his head. Just beneath it, the gold altar that Luca told me about.

And in front of it...

Jack Donovan.

He grips the edge of his desk, too late to hide the angry expression he had on while talking to the other woman. A flash of annoyance does little to replace it as he addresses Luca's dad with a terse, "Yes, Frank?"

Frank. Frank St. James.

I was right!

He bows his head. "Apologies, prophet. I didn't realize you were with your wife."

Huh. My head shoots back to her. Me, neither.

Emily. That's Emily.

Luca's Emily.

Damn it. She's *beautiful*.

Oh, she's slightly worn down, though having three

kids under four by the time you're in your mid-twenties might do that to you. The loose dress hanging off of her isn't doing her any favors, either. She still has a natural beauty that shines through regardless, and a lingering spirit in the way she was glaring at her husband as we walked in that tells me she'll be okay after I'm done.

I turn my attention from the woman back to the ostentatious figure standing behind the desk.

I look closer this time. Emily is in her mid-twenties. Donovan is at least sixty. His skin is that fake orange-y color you get when you think you'll look better with a tan, and his hair is quite obviously a black toupee that gives new meaning to 'rug'. Seriously. Did someone cut a piece of shag carpet and drop it on top of his bald head?

He's a thick, round man with dark, watery, beady eyes that turn immediately lecherous when he sees me standing just behind Luca's father.

"What's this?" he asks.

"A new member for the fold."

I step around Mr. St. James, walking toward the desk. At my approach, Emily moves to the side.

Her husband doesn't notice. He's too busy leering at me.

Ugh.

"You Jack Donovan?"

"Yes, I am, child. How can I serve you?"

I shrug. "You can die."

His haughty expression turns puzzled, almost as if he can't believe he heard what he did. "Excuse me?"

"No," I say cheerily. "I don't think I will."

And then, to make it obvious that I'm not kidding, I dip my hand in my jacket and pull out the Ruger. I aim it at him.

The fucker moves.

That's the problem with being a bloated bastard in your late sixties. You don't move as fast as you used to, and as Donovan breaks for his wife as though he has every intention of trying to hide his bulk behind her, it only takes a second for me to readjust my aim before I fire.

I get him dead in the chest before he can reach Emily and the baby. Because my aim is, as ever, fucking perfect, it's a kill shot. He gurgles as he hits the ground, then goes instantly silent.

He's the only one who does.

Emily screams. Because her mother is screaming, the baby cries.

Luca's father stares in horror as he shouts nonsense that I tune out.

Ignoring the noise, I march around the desk and put another bullet through Donovan's brain for good measure.

I'm sure the two shots ringing out will catch the rest of the settlement's attention. Now that I did the first part of what I came here to do, it's time I finish up and catch the next flight out to Florida like I planned.

But first, I give Mr. St. James an appraising look.

On my way over, I thought about eliminating his parents if I had the chance. Donovan was my main target, but if I could find them... they'd be excellent candidates for my special type of justice, too. For fuck's sake, they *branded* Luca. They twisted him up over his sexuality, and sat back as this creep preyed on a girl young enough to be all of their daughters. When Luca tried to save her, they disowned him, only attempting to bring him back to their fold when the precious prophet told them to.

A man of God? Hell, no. Between the golden church, the golden altar, and the diamond-encrusted cross hanging in this office, he couldn't be further from the truth. He's a con man. A cheat. A chea*ter*.

A fraud.

And now he's dead.

By some stroke of luck, I found Luca's father. I should kill him, too. He'd deserve it, but you know what? That would be too easy. Let him know that his son escaped. That he found a partner who is willing to kill for him.

That he's living a good life working for a man called Devil while they worship a false prophet who tried to use his own wife and child as a human shield when he saw my gun...

So I don't kill him. Leaving him to live this sorry existence without Luca? That's justice enough.

Giving him a dismissive look while still clutching

my gun, I move toward the wall. Stepping over Donovan's corpse, I ignore the way that Emily's scream becomes a gasp as she rushes out of my reach.

Not like I was heading toward her anyway. I just needed to get a little closer, then to jump a little higher, and— yes! I've snatched the diamond cross off the wall.

"I'll be taking this with me, thank you."

Emily nods abruptly, as if giving me permission.

Hiding on the other side of the room, Mr. St. James points a trembling finger at me. "You can't do that!"

Watch me.

"Who do you think you are?" demands Luca's father. "Stop this instant!"

"Me?" I hook the thumb on my free hand through a loop in my jeans. The other taps against the butt of my gun. "I'm the Hummingbird. And unless you want me coming back here, you'll forget you ever saw me. And if I *do* come back? I'll take the rest of Donavan down with me."

I'm banking on these cultish idiots seeing how easily I killed their precious leader and realizing that if his 'faith' couldn't save him, they don't have a chance. To be fair, I should just shoot them all now. Bam. Bam. Bam. When I remember the brutal scar on Luca's arm, my trigger finger twitches. And Emily...

I shift my weight, swiveling the barrel of the Ruger from Luca's father to Luca's ex.

She pales, hugging her infant close to her chest,

shielding as much of the small body with her own as she can.

I lower the gun.

"Find a better husband," I tell her, a tiny bit of remorse tugging on my heartstrings. For all I know, Donovan was Emily's Jason. Though, if that was the case, then I did her a favor by killing that cheating POS...

However, before she gets any ideas in that pretty blonde head of hers, I make sure to add: "But not Luca. He's *mine*."

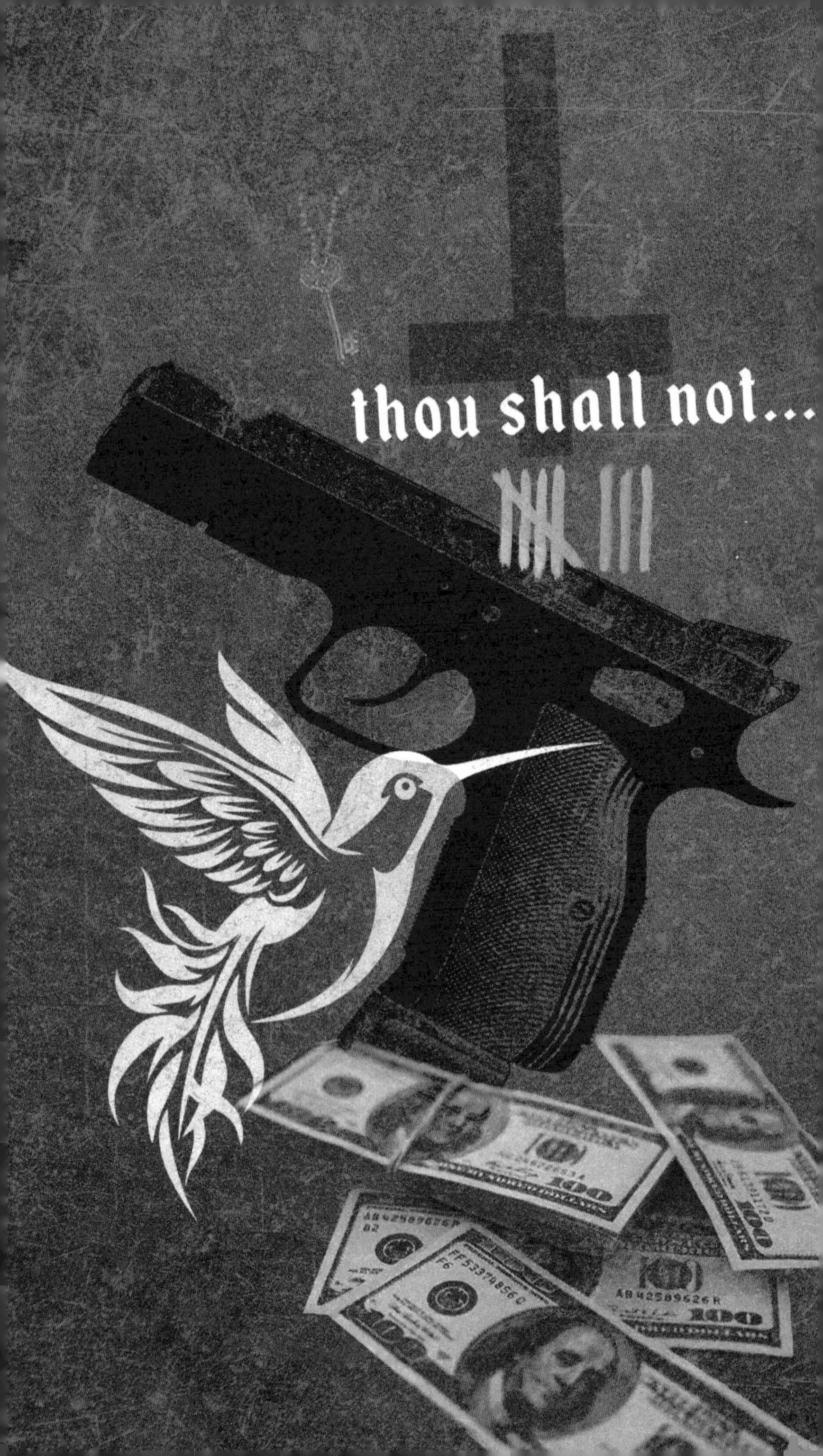
thou shall not...

TWENTY-TWO
REUNITED

LUCA

In Springfield, when one enemy disappears, another is quick to take its place.

That's what comes of being a well-known criminal hotspot. When the lawless *are* the law, it's obvious that those looking to profit will challenge those at the top.

First, it was the Libellula Family and the Sinners Syndicate at odds. They were uneasy compatriots, then fierce rivals, and finally allies as the two largest gangs in Springfield found a reason to stop fighting each other.

And, sure, that reason was Damien Libellula using Devil's love for his wife against him, but after Cross fell for Damien's baby sister, the uneasy truce became something a little stronger. Something a lot more unbreakable. They still own the East End. Us Sinners control the West Side. Together, we are Springfield.

And the Snowflakes are fucking over.

Of course, that just means that Falco has decided to start shit now that there's an opening for pricks who want to give Devil a hard time...

Still, Johnny Winter *is* dead. It's barely been a week since Kylie used the burner phone to shoot over the pic of Winter's body on the floor, her faithful strychnine going to work on the man. True, it wasn't the explosive end he deserved—and I hate to ask what he did with the C4 she brought with her to their meet—but as she added in her last message before she ditched the burner, a man who spent his life working from the shadows in the hope that everyone would know his name deserved to die without any effort.

That's my Hummingbird.

That's my girl.

At least... I thought she was mine.

It's been a week. That was the last anyone has heard from her, and while she told me to expect that, I went from spending every minute of every day with her in Burns's cabin to *nothing*. For twenty-seven years, I slept alone. For mere days, I curled up behind Kylie. Going back to an empty bed was fucking torture, even though she promised that she'd be back before I knew it.

That was the plan. The Hummingbird is quick. She's always in motion. Banking on the fact that

Winter wouldn't be alone, that his bodyguards would've at least had an idea who he was meeting with, she needed to fly the coop once it was obvious she killed Winter.

She's a contract killer. A hired hitman—well, like she says, a hit*woman*. In this biz, loyalty stays in-house. The criminal world would understand that money talks. If she got a higher price on Winter's head, they'd respect that she'd turn on her former employer. She didn't owe him anything since he hadn't completed payment. It's just *business*.

No one paid Kylie to take down Winter. In fact, she did it pro bono as a way to prove to Devil that she wasn't a liability. Because while Kylie was never loyal to her clients, somehow I did what I doubted I ever could do : I got her to love me.

Her loyalty. It's *mine*.

It *has* to be.

Right?

Fuck!

My thoughts distracted, my head wishing it was between Kylie's thighs instead of bowing over my toolbox, I toss the socket in my hand. I'd been meaning to grab a 7/32, but I picked up a 9/32 instead. A stupid mistake, and I curse under my breath as I root around for the right one.

Seven days. It's been seven days, and she promised me that she'd only be in Florida for five.

I knew she had plans to visit her family in the new

year. Needing to lie low a little in case Winter's shaken crew decide to come after her, she bumped up the trip. As soon as Winter went down, the plan was for Kylie to head right for the nearest airport. Five days in Florida, then she'd return to Springfield.

Return to *me*.

I believed her. From the start, I never lied to her. I can't say the same for her, but considering the situation she was in, I forgive her for protecting her identity. For protecting her intentions. It was her or me, and she didn't know Luca St. James at all then.

She knows me now. And maybe we jumped into everything too fast, but it just... it felt *right*. Like she was the one I was meant to suffer through life to find. My reward. She *loves* me, and I keep telling myself that as I strip the lug nut I'm trying to remove.

Devil was supposed to go see *Romeo and Juliet* tonight. Genevieve is Juliet in this season's ballet, and I planned on being on duty so that I could drive Devil and his wife out to Riverside to see the performance.

I would've. This is still my job. I'm even more loyal to the boss than before after how I got so close to Kylie because of him, one way or another. But knowing that I was invited, too, and that Cross even got a ticket for Kylie to show there were no hard feelings over the fire... shit. No wonder the socket wrench was giving me trouble. I picked up a 7/32 again.

Damn it.

Working on my '67 Ford Mustang was supposed to

take my mind off of how much I fucking miss my Kylie. I haven't been down to the garage to continue restoring it since before the fateful night when I dropped Devil off to have dinner with Damien Libellula.

That's where he is tonight. After a young Sinner got gunned down by one of Falco's men, Rolls, Devil, Damien, and Vincent Libellula are meeting to discuss how best to shut this latest threat to Springfield down.

I should've been the one to bring the boss across the city. That's my job, but he went in Rolls's car while I've been fucking around with this tire for the last half an hour.

That's on me. Last night, I ran two red lights on the way back to Paradise Suites. So out of the ordinary for me, Devil decided that I needed a break from being behind the wheels. I tried to argue that I just had one —I didn't drive those weeks I was upstate with Kylie— but when Devil gives you an order, you listen.

So here I am. Pacing around my apartment, obsessing over where Kylie was and what she was doing... it wasn't helping. Tending to my Mustang was supposed to take my mind off of her, but not only do my fingers seem to have stopped working, but why the hell does it feel like someone's looking over my shoulder?

My head snaps behind me. Out of the corner of my eye, I see the shadow, but when I turn, that pretty face with the amused smirk has me dropping from one knee to both before landing on my elbow.

I hit the concrete floor of the garage, but I barely notice the ache as Kylie's eyes twinkle in the dim lighting.

"Miss me, ace?"

I lash my hand out, grabbing her arm. I was right when I suspected someone was peeking over my shoulder. While I was struggling with the damn socket wrench, she must've snuck up behind me, crouching down at my back, waiting for me to notice her.

There's a duffel bag at her feet. Her hair is wild and loose, a pair of unnecessary sunglasses tucking the curls out of her face. A souvenir from her trip to Florida? Maybe, but it doesn't matter. She's back.

She's *here*.

I tug on her at the same as I pull myself into a seated position. Kylie's laugh is a balm on my lonely soul as she allows herself to land in my lap.

Wrapping my arms around her, squeezing her tight so that she can't escape me, I find her lips with mine and kiss her until we're both breathless. Then, when I'm afraid that she's running out of air, I pull back, nuzzling her soft cheek with my nose.

She smells *amazing*.

Fuck, I missed her. Let her go? I'll never be able to let her go.

She wants to go back to Florida, I'm there. Might as well meet the parents since she'll have to kill me before I allow us to be separated for a whole fucking *week* ever again. She needs a place to stay now that she's back?

It'll be here. She needs a job if she's serious about retiring as the Hummingbird? There's always something the Sinners need, and she's as resourceful as she is smart and fearless.

But, more than that, she's mine—and the fact that she's here, in my arms, proves it.

Kylie tucks her arms under my pits, completing our embrace. "That answers my question for me, huh? Not like I don't appreciate the welcome, but you act like I went to Mars instead of Florida."

As far out of my reach as it was, it might as well have been Mars.

"Five days," I growl.

She pats my back. "Right. I went to Florida for five days."

"It's been a week!"

"No one said I couldn't make a pit stop first."

I pull away from her. "A pit stop? What do you mean, a pit stop?"

She pauses, her forehead furrowing. "How pissed will you be if I tell you that I changed my flight? Then booked the Florida one for the next day?"

My forehead furrows. "What do you mean?"

I get an impish smile in return. "So... about my job. Remember how I said I'll still kill sometimes, especially to keep you from it?"

I nod, my stomach twisting. "Baby, baby... Kylie. No. Don't tell me you went after Cross after all."

When was the last time I talked to him? I've been

lying low in the apartment's parking garage so... shit. He told me about the tickets a couple of days ago. She couldn't have—

She blinks, confused. "Wait? The artist?" A shake of her head has the knots in my guts unraveling. "No. I had a bigger target in mind. And before you look like you're gonna shit yourself again, I'll tell you it wasn't the Devil of Springfield, either."

I'm glad to hear it. But if it wasn't two of Kylie's only failed contracts, then *who*?

I get the answer a moment later when she wiggles off my lap, taking perverse enjoyment as she gives my cock a possessive stroke before she pops up, walking over to the duffel bag she abandoned. She drops down — I swallow a groan when she shows off her ass—and unzips the bag.

I lick my lips. I'm already fantasizing about bending her over my bed, christening it as *ours* by fucking her ass if she'll let me, and the memory of how good it felt to thrust into that tight heat has me too distracted to realize that she pulled a black bag out of the duffel.

With one hand, she gestures for me to get to my feet. There isn't anything I won't do for Kylie, even something as simple as that. I push myself up until I'm standing, and once I do, she hands it to me.

I lift my eyebrows.

Her hands slip into the pockets of her jeans as she

rocks on her heels. "So... my pit stop? Was in Oklahoma."

Another knot returns to my anxious gut. That happens whenever I think of my hometown and the shit I left behind after I fled Donovan... but why would she go there?

Unless...

"Kylie. You *didn't*—"

Her eyes twinkle in amusement. "Oh, ace. I *did*. Brought you back a souvenir, too."

From Oklahoma.

What would she—

"Go on," she says encouragingly. "Open it up."

I do.

Whatever's in the bag, it's deceptively heavy. Once the bag is open, I tip it into my waiting palm.

The diamond-encrusted cross sparkles in the garage's fluorescent lights.

Holy fucking shit.

I don't even have to ask. I know exactly who her target was.

Jack Donovan.

thou shall not...

TWENTY-THREE
HUSBAND

KYLIE

I hold my breath.

Over the years, I've lost track of how many people I've killed. Maybe that sounds cold. Callous. It's the job. Once I started taking payments for the lives I took, it became a game. I barely remember any of the victories while stewing over my rare failures.

No wonder Luca suspected I might've taken the opportunity to close my books before I retire. Nah. I'm not worried about that.

But revenge? Fuck, yeah. I'm always up for a little revenge.

Just like how I killed Jason Villa because of how he treated my sister, when I realized that I considered Luca St. James one of the few who belonged to me, no way in hell was I going to let those people who terrorized him get away with it.

He knows. The moment he recognizes the cross I gave him, he has to know that I went all the way to Oklahoma just to take it from that Donavan dickhead.

But I'm not a thief. I wouldn't go all the way there just to steal, but if I reappropriated it from the man I killed... that's definitely more my style.

And while I'm pretty sure that Luca knows that, that doesn't stop him from staring at the cross for a few seconds before he glances at me and asks, "How did you—"

"Oh." Maybe I have to be a little more clear. "Yeah. I killed that orange freak. Then I took it."

I hold my breath again, waiting.

Luca's handsome splits into a wide grin. "He was orange, wasn't he? I always wondered if he went tanning on the congregation's dime."

"Spray tan, definitely." And a shitty one, too. "The blood on his chest was a big improvement."

Still clutching the diamond, though I have his entire attention, he says softly, "I want to hear everything. Please, baby."

I could suggest that we go up to his apartment. I stayed there a couple of days while waiting for New Year's so I know where it is. We'd have more privacy there, but the garage is empty, and the way he's using a pet name for me has me melting already. He wants to hear all the bloody details on how I took down the prophet who fucked up his life?

I'm happy to oblige.

When I'm done, his mouth is slightly open. "You did it in front of Emily? And my dad?"

"I let him come along on purpose," I admit. "The guy looked like an older version of you, only more... pinched." I wrinkle my nose. "I figured he had to be your dad. It was just a touch of poetic justice that he was in the room when I pulled the trigger. Same as how it was that dickhead's office where it all went down. I saw the gold altar he hid in there. I figured the diamond cross would be in there, but he actually had it hanging on the wall over his head. Tacky as fuck, but at least it saved me time trying to figure out where to find it. The second I saw it, though? I knew I had to get it and give it to you."

And that's not all...

Luca rubs his thumb over the cut gems. "Donovan is finally dead. Good fucking riddance, though I guess I'm not surprised I didn't hear about it. That cult is so small, so secluded, they're probably still gathered around his body, waiting to see if he'll rise like Jesus."

I shrug. "Maybe. Or maybe I told them that I'd come back with some more C4 and blow the whole fucking church up if they even think about retaliating." With a laugh, I add, "It's a lot easier to intimidate sheep than it is to be a Hummingbird among Sinners and Dragonflies, I'll tell you that."

He chokes. "You did that?"

"Sure did. Made sure to mention that anyone who already left that hellhole was off-limits, too. Especially you, ace." I poke him in the chest. "Said the same thing to Emily. I killed her husband. Told her to find a new one, but she needed to stay away from *mine*."

Luca winces at the mention of Emily, but his eyes are searching my face for some sign that I'm screwing with him by the time I'm done claiming him.

"You called me your husband?" he says softly.

I plan to make him my husband, too.

But, first—

Reaching into my pocket, I pull out one black box, give it a shake, then shove it back into the pocket. "Hang on. Wrong box." Dipping into the other pocket, I find the larger black box. "Ah. Here it is." I toss it to Luca. "Something else for you, ace."

"What is it?"

"Open it. You'll see."

He flips the lid, then pulls out the silver chain. Hanging off the end of it is a key completely different from the one he has on. It reminds me of the cheap, little metal key I got with this teen diary I bought from the dollar store a million years ago, only a little thicker.

He holds it up, a question written in every line of his face.

I shrug. "I could say some sappy shit, like it's the key to my heart. That's not my style. I love you. I *picked* you. I'll hunt you down if you try to leave me... and if you don't know that means you own every part of my twisted soul, then I don't know what to tell you. I could've killed you in five different ways before you even lied to me about your name, but I didn't, and *I* should've known then that I was in over my head. It is what it is, and that means you're mine." I raise my eyebrows. "Right?"

His smile forms, a little goofy, and, *fuck*, I love it. "Right."

Good. "Anyway... I know that key you wear means a lot to you. Now that we have the cross, I don't see why you need to wear it anymore, so I got you a replacement.

"It goes to a safe deposit box. Since it looks like we're sticking around in Springfield, I got one at the First Bank off Willow Ave. You're not flashy enough to walk around with a six-inch diamond-encrusted cross. With that devil on your arm, someone would have to be an idiot to try to rob you. But, way I figure it, you got used to wearing a key, and I'd rather it be one I gave you."

"Kylie... I don't know what to say."

I meet his gaze, too cocky to allow myself to be rejected. "Then don't say anything. But, if you would, swap it for the old one."

Luca doesn't even reach up to unclasp the chain he's worn these last five years. Without breaking our stare, he grabs the chain. With a twist, it's broken. The useless key to an altar states away skitters to the ground as he gently places the new chain with the safe deposit key around his neck.

Once he has, I decide to go full hog. I might have said that I'm not about to say anything all that sappy, but I did. It was sappy and it was possessive, and it was perfect for what I'm about to do now.

I know which pocket has the other box. I grab it, and with a wink, I toss that one at Luca next.

"Another gift?"

Luca starts to tug on the top.

"Don't open it yet," I tell him.

He lets the lid close with a soft *snap*.

"Put it in your pocket." I wait until he does, then I add, "Listen. I'm gonna fuck you one day. For real. The way you count it as fucking. See, now, that means I gotta marry you, ace. But just so that you don't think I'm so fucked-up, I'll promise you forever just to get laid, that's the ring I want when you're ready."

He pats his pocket. "You bought yourself an engagement ring?"

I shrug. "I know what I like. And I like you."

Luca lifts his hand, cupping my cheek. "No. You love me. And I've never wanted a woman like I want you. I don't just mean sex, either. I want *you*. You're the most fascinating person I've ever met. You want me to get down on one knee? I'll do it right now."

I plant my hand on his chest. "Surprise me. Like I said, when you're ready... when you realize that I'm the type of woman who only commits once, and I fucking mean it when I say until death do us part... ask me then. I'm not in any rush. I'm not going anywhere, either."

Going up on my tiptoes, I press my lips against his.

And then I smile.

"I'm yours. No chains required."

thou shall not...

EPILOGUE

KYLIE

FOUR MONTHS LATER

There's no rest for the wicked—or a semi-retired hitwoman, either.

It's my fault. I promised Luca that we'd have a phone-free day. It wasn't a big deal. After two weeks in the cabin, I got used to going without it. It was actually a bit of a relief, not having that sucker glued to my hand all the time. Sure, I had to do some backtracking after we left it, including getting a new one to replace the phone the hotel 'lost' out of the locked safe while I was gone, but in case me and Luca didn't work out, I wanted to keep my rep intact. If I wanted to keep my books open, I needed a way for my prospective clients to get in touch.

In Springfield, the Sinners and the Dragonflies took full credit for ending Johnny Winter and his criminal enterprise. Outside of the city, I slapped my name on it. The Hummingbird blew up part of the Devil's Playground *and* manipulated the head of the Snowflakes into his own demise. Not to mention, whispers of Jack Donovan's death made its way to my network.

I've never been more in demand, even after the Devil of Springfield seemingly rose from the dead.

I've stuck to my semi-retired status, though. And not because I let Luca brainwash me into thinking 'thou shall not kill'. Please. It's just... I was having way more fun planning my wedding than plotting to take out another target.

And because Kylie plans and plans well, it went off without a hitch.

I had almost three months to come up with my vision and execute it. Though, to be honest, I started figuring out what I wanted to do the moment I bought my own engagement ring. Secretly, I gave Luca until the end of January to be on one knee, offering my ring back and his hand in marriage.

He made it ten days.

When it's right, it's right, and fucking hell, what the two of us have is *right*. I don't question it. That's not my style. I just do what feels good, and having a courthouse wedding with Lincoln 'Devil' Crewes and his sweet wife, Ava, serving as our witnesses earlier this afternoon was the best kind of wedding I could have.

I'll have to tell my parents I got married. Lindy will be pissed she couldn't be here, but I'll make it up to them. After they meet Luca and fall in love with him the same way that I have, we'll do the whole she-bang down in Florida.

Luca tried to get me to agree to do that now. And, honestly, for the first two and a half months, I started to plan a big wedding for the two of us. Then we both quickly realized that, for some of the things I wanted, the wait list was super far out. Like, some of the vendors wanted to book us for next year.

Luca has held firm on his 'saving himself for marriage' stance; of course, that's a lot easier when he can fuck my ass whenever he wants to. But I know he's been dying to stick his cock in me. He made it the three months before he started to waver, and that's when I decided to hell with the whole wedding thing.

In three days, our courthouse ceremony was planned, and it only took that long because the stupid law said we needed to wait seventy-two hours to use our wedding license. As of an hour ago, I consider myself Kylie St. James, even if I still have to go through the trouble of changing my maiden name.

Bureaucrats.

Either way, I'm married now. And my horny husband is waiting in our bathroom for me to slip out of the simple white wedding dress I had him buy me for just the occasion.

Only that's not what I'm doing, is it? Instead, I snuck my phone into the bathroom with me because I noticed the notifications coming in through the burner app on my phone and knew someone was reaching out to the Hummingbird.

Ignoring the unfamiliar number at the top, I read the messages:

> June deadline

> Desmond James

> Harmony Heights

> 150k

> Adrian H

I whistle. One-hundred-fifty grand to off a single guy before June? It's a two-month window, so it's definitely doable, even with my scheduled honeymoon starting tomorrow. I don't know who this Desmond James is, or why Adrian H is willing to pay that much to see him dead, but I'm not in the right mood to look into it.

Without a reason to catch my flighty attention, I pass on jobs. However, I'm still a petty bitch at heart. Even if I'm Kylie St. James now instead of the Hummingbird, some things never change.

And with a coy smile on my face, I screenshot the

message and forward it to Nicholas Reed.

But not before I use an app I have to change the word 'June' in the first message to 'July'.

He wants to get all in my business because the Hummingbird was taking too many contracts away from the Reed twins? Fine. I had Luca get Nicholas Reed's phone number from Devil, and in a bid to show the head Sinner that I was willing to work with his syndicate and his associates, I started passing on the jobs I rejected to Nicholas and Hunter Reed.

Sometimes, they're legit offers. And, sometimes, I fuck with them just to make life difficult for the nosy Nicholas.

June deadline? What do you mean, June? Your message clearly said July... and since he'll have the doctored screenshot, and the burner app erases texts in twenty-four hours, they'll both think they're right, and no one will suspect the Hummingbird.

They never do...

But, for now, I'm not the Hummingbird. I'm Kylie.

I'm Luca's wife.

And, as I toss my phone on top of the stack of towels by his sink—*our* sink—I smile.

Because I'm going to go fuck my husband.

I TOLD LUCA THAT HE HAD TO WAIT IN THE LIVING ROOM while I 'freshened' up. True, I did a little work before tossing my phone in the sink, then leaving my panties on the bathroom floor, but I needed to set up a few things before I was ready for our wedding night.

Poor guy. Over the last few months, I've heard a couple of stories about his job. He's still Devil's personal driver—and the amount of hours he spends away from the apartment is one reason why I'm semi-retired and not completely retired because I get so fucking *bored*—and though the Sinners have my loyalty now, I'm not a Sinner. To save Luca from having to struggle about who owns *his* loyalty, I don't ask questions, and I accept that there are things that are mafia biz that he can't tell me about.

If I pushed it? He'd fold to make me happy. Just knowing that is enough so I don't push it unless it has something to do with my speciality.

Or if it's funny.

I like the funny stories.

But Luca... though he's adorably close-mouthed when it comes to details, he makes it obvious that the Devil of Springfield and his wife have a bit of a kinky side of their own. They often have 'alone time' when they're not actually alone; as the driver, he's had to tune out whatever the hell has Ava Crewes squealing her husband's name in the backseat.

We took Luca's Mustang to the courthouse, and though it's a four-seater, I wasn't about to let him fuck me the second the justice of the peace pronounced us married. Especially when Ava choked a little when I prodded my new husband in his chest and told him that he could wait until we got home to consummate our marriage.

Besides, I have a *plan*.

Reaching into my 'go' bag, I grab the toy handcuffs I bought online. Luca didn't have a headboard attached to his bed when I moved myself in. Shit, he was squeezing himself on a twin. I helped him upgrade to a queen-sized bed—and, knowing that I had every intention of getting *some* payback on him, I picked the perfect headboard for our wedding night.

I hook one cuff around a center bar, then tuck it under the pillow so that Luca won't see it. The small container I prepped goes in the side table drawer. The 'go' bag gets tossed under the bed before I proclaim myself ready.

I'm not the only one.

Knock, knock.

"Kylie? I'm getting lonely out here, baby. Can I come in yet?"

I love that he asks. Like, fucking *love* it. So many of these mafia men would just kick in the door, heft me up, toss me on the bed, and have their way with me. And while I've gotten Luca to act that way toward me when I'm in the mood to be possessed, he's learned the very enjoyable lesson that I'm willing to let him do anything to me—as long as he hands over control when *I* want it.

And on our wedding night when I crave creating a

memory to replace his twisted outlook on sex? That's definitely one of them.

Luca is no shy virgin. Not anymore. Despite his hang-ups—and, I tell you, I still have the urge to go back to Oklahoma and hunt down his parents—he's come a long way since we got together.

Since the cabin, he's had my ass. He's fucked me with his tongue. I've sucked him off so much, I started to refer to his cock as my favorite lollipop. His fingers have been inside me. But his dick...

He wanted to save himself for marriage. Twenty-one years of brainwashing had him convinced that, if he poked a pussy with his dick before some higher authority proclaimed us married, he'd go to hell.

Murder? As long as it wasn't the tenth command-ment he broke, that was fine. But premarital sex? Heaven forbid... though, at the same time, I shouldn't be snarky when his repressed upbringing means that I will never have to worry about him cheating on me.

Thou shall not commit adultery.

He's Luca. *My* Luca. He won't be like Jack Donovan.

Cheating or murder? Luca will follow in Devil's footsteps way before he does the prophet that no one seems to care about—or remember in the months following his death. And if I cheated, I'd be an asshole.

And, semi-retired or not, I still live to eliminate assholes.

Tonight, though? I'm not the Hummingbird. I'm

Kylie St. James, and I fluff out the skirt of my wedding dress as I call back, "Go ahead."

The second we made it back to the apartment, Luca was already shedding clothing. He left his suit jacket in the backseat of the Mustang. The tie he wore —because he insisted that he wear a suit and tie for our courthouse wedding—was tossed on the couch. He kicked off his shoes. His button-down shirt was halfway unbuttoned before I hurried into the bathroom, leaving him pacing the living room.

As he walks in, I see that Luca finished undressing while he waited. My tongue darts out, dabbing the corner of my mouth as he stalks in, stroking his cock in barely concealed impatience.

It's a nice dick. I've seen my fair share, and even if he isn't my husband, I'd still give him a thumbs up. Sure, I was a little nervous the first time that he'd fit inside my ass, but now I know better. If I can take him there, my pussy is going to be a breeze.

My body is already responding. Just being around Luca is enough to get my engine revving—and, to be honest, part of me wanted to push him back into the driver's seat, heft up my skirts, and sink down on top of him right after the wedding. The only thing holding me back was knowing this is, in Luca's eyes, his first time.

I'm his wife now. I'm going to make this fucking *memorable*.

Of course, I need my own fun. I need to enjoy

myself. I love this guy, but I'm no saint. I just take the fantasy I had and switch it up a little. Instead of the driver's seat, I plan on taking him right on our new bed.

But first—

If he's surprised that I haven't stripped like he has, he doesn't say anything. As I've gotten to know Luca, he's made it his purpose to learn everything about me, too. Me choosing to bang him in my wedding dress? Yeah, that's a pretty 'me' thing to do.

Just like meeting him in the middle of the room, kissing him deeply before goosing his ass, then pushing him in the small of his back toward the bed is, too.

"Get on," I order, my voice throaty and provocative.

Luca climbs on top of the mattress, flipping over so that he's sitting with his back up against the headboard.

Perfect.

Hefting up the skirts of my wedding dress, I throw my leg over both of his, straddling him. With my legs spread—and without any underwear on—my hot, wet pussy drag across his muscular thigh.

Luca throws his head back against the wall, eyes momentarily closed as the anticipation runs through both of us.

I almost forgot what I intended to do. Being this close to taking him for the first time, it's instinctive to search for his cock and feed it inside of me. Only knowing that it'll be that much more explosive—for the both of us—if I go ahead with my vision for our wedding night has me ignoring the erection searching for me in favor of snatching the cheap metal tucked beneath the pillow.

Where is it?

Where is it—

Yes!

I snatch it, hurriedly snapping it around Luca's wrist at the exact moment he senses that something is up.

Luca gulps, deep green eyes darkening in a mix of lust and sudden worry as they pop back open. "Uh, Kylie?"

"Yeah, ace?"

"What happened to my hand?"

I give him the most innocent expression I can muster. "What's the matter? Not a fan of having your hand attached to the headboard?"

Stroking the edge of his jaw, trailing my finger down the side of his throat before resting my palm between his pecs, I smile at him. "Lucky for you, I'm just keeping you where I want you before I give you the ride of your life."

His Adam's apple bobs. "I've been waiting for you to get back at me," he admits. "I guess this is better than poison."

I wink at him. "See? I thought you'd agree. Besides, I know you. If I let you have both hands, you'll want to touch me. No. Not yet. Because tonight? This is about *you*."

Luca shudders. "It's our wedding night. You and me."

"Oh, I know. Maybe I should rephrase that. Tonight *is* ours, and I'm sure you'll make me come as many times as I want. But for the first time? I want to focus on you. Sound like a plan?"

My husband stretches his arm over his head, grabbing the top of the headboard with the hand already cuffed to the center bar.

I guess I have my answer.

Adjusting the skirts with one hand so that my ass is out and my pussy bare, I use my other hand to grip Luca's dick by the base.

His whole body stiffens.

The tip of my tongue peeks through the gap in my teeth as I tease, "Nice to have two hands, isn't it?"

"Even nicer," he pants, a slight vein in his neck bulging as though it's taking everything he has not to start bucking wildly, "if you use your hand to put me where I belong."

"Oh? And where's that, Mr. St. James?"

"In my wife's pussy. That way, she *is* my wife."

Please. I know he'll only consider us truly wed when we fuck—sorry, consummate the marriage—but even if I gave him blue balls and told him we had to wait until I was in the mood, he's still my husband.

Like I warned Emily in that church, he's *mine*.

But he's also super fucking lucky because, with this man, I'm constantly in the mood. I might have a little more fun continuing to tease him, but with my pussy fucking weeping with how much I've waited for this, I'd only be torturing myself if I held out any longer.

Rising up on my knees, I angle Luca's dick until it finds the entrance to my waiting heat. I'm slick as fuck, which makes it easy for me to swallow him whole.

Sinking down on him, letting my weight carry me until our groins are flush, I let the skirts fall as Luca's eyes go dazed.

I swivel my hips, making sure I've taken him all. "How's that feel, ace?"

"You've killed me," he croaks.

"What's that?"

With his free hand, he finds my waist through the fabric of my wedding dress. "You had to have. You killed me... put fucking poison on your lips before you kissed me... 'cause I have to be a dead man. This is Heaven. I never want to leave."

Isn't he sweet? Delusional, but sweet.

God, I fucking love him.

"So, you telling me not to move?" Another experimental swivel, putting a little more oomph into it as I squeeze my inner muscles. "'Cause it's better when I move."

"Fuck me—"

"I'm trying, Luca."

A rumble in his throat. "That's not what I meant."

I swallow my laugh. "It's not?"

"Kylie…"

I lift up, then fall on him.

"Kylie!"

"That's more like it, ace." Starting out slowly, just so he can sense the difference in the motion, I begin to bounce.

For a moment, he can't even speak. He pants, moans, huffs out my name, plus a blasphemous prayer to a God he no longer believes in to give him the strength to hold out as long as he can, but what would be the fun in that? If there's anything that gives me enjoyment—besides, you know, getting to come myself —it's seeing him lose complete control.

I can already tell that the sensation of fucking a different part of me is too much for him. Luca gets this focused look on his face whenever he's getting ready to explode, and I can see it now as he starts tugging on the handcuff.

"Let me have my hand," he begs. "I need to fucking touch you. I need to make you come."

"Don't worry about that. I'll get mine." I always do, and Luca knows it. Even more importantly, my lover isn't a selfish one. He's always determined to give me pleasure, reveling in a sense of pride that he wrenches multiple Os out of me. "But first… I want to make *you* come."

I rock back and forth on his length, trying to get a little friction going against my clit; I mean, if I *do* happen to come, I won't complain. My breath comes a little faster. Luca's look of pure devotion has endorphins flooding through me, making me feel like I'm flying high even as I ride him.

His free hand lands on my tit. Even through the thick material of the dress, I sense the tips of his fingers as he squeezes me—so I squeeze him.

Luca held out longer than I thought, but that last one does it. Bucking up into me, grunting my name as he fills me up with everything he has, I'm not even riding him anymore. I mean, shit. I'm just holding on for dear life as he slams up again, keeping us connected while he finishes.

When he's done, I'm almost as out of breath as he is. I'm not completely unsatisfied—which makes me wonder if there was a pop of pleasure, a frisson of release I didn't notice, so in tune with Luca's need instead—though that could also be because I plan on fucking this man all night long.

And the rest of my life, too.

Forever. He promised me forever, and that's exactly what I'm going to expect from him—

"Um, baby?"

"Hm?"

I'd sprawled out on his chest once he stopped thrusting up. Between plotting the wedding, throwing the plans we had away, setting up the courthouse wedding, and now giving my new husband what *he* needed, I'm fucking exhausted.

He shakes his wrist, drawing my attention to the cuff still keeping his arm stretched over his head.

Oh. Right.

I should probably free him now, huh?

Easing up slowly into a sitting position, grinning as Luca groans when this new position takes his cock with me as I scoot a little closer to him and the head-board. The groan turns pained as he slips out of me, but he doesn't have to worry. I'll get his hand out of the cuff, then he can go back to doing whatever he wants to me.

Hey. It's only fair since I got to do what I wanted to *him...*

Dipping my head quick enough to steal a kiss from my slightly dazed husband, I reach up, unhooking the hoop earring I wore to get married today. It's the same hoop earring that I always wear—a gift from Lindy the Christmas after Jason's death, I never change them—and it's just as easy to trigger the locking mechanism on the handcuff tonight as it was when he put them on me.

It pops off in less than five seconds. Smirking down at him, I slip my earring back into place on my lobe.

"So that's how you did it," he marvels with a laugh.

I preen. "I'm a woman of many talents."

"Oh, trust me, I know." His eyes light up. "Even better, you're my wife."

Considering I'm full of his come, I guess I really am now in his eyes...

"Like I said when I made my vows to you in front of God and the Devil, it's 'til death do us part, ace." I boop his nose. "And don't forget. I'm a hitwoman."

I *know* death.

But, who knows, maybe it's time to live a little?

I plan on it. No more death wish for me. With Luca at my side, there's so much I want to do. So much I want to see. For now, though, I like the idea of having a home. This apartment has slowly become ours over the last few months, and I look forward to a future with this man.

Shit. I look forward to him recovering so that we can begin round two...

I've grown to know Luca's body. He's gotten better at lasting, though we both went into this expecting him to go off quickly if only because he's been waiting so fucking long to feel a pussy working his dick. I give him ten more minutes before he reverses our positions, putting me under him.

So why not have a snack?

I start to scoot off of him, pausing when he grabs a handful of lace.

"Where are you going, Mrs. St. James? I'm not done with you."

"I'm not going too far. I just..." Without him releasing the skirt of my wedding dress, I have to stretch to reach the side table. Pulling open the drawer, I grab the container I shoved in there. I give it a quick shake before flicking the lid open. It lands on the floor, but I barely pay attention as I grab one of the pale green cubes inside.

"Want a cuke?"

Luca bursts into laughter as he shakes his head. The pure joy in the sound makes cutting the cucumber, putting it into a container, and carrying that around with me all afternoon just to see his reaction all worth it.

I eat one. It's slimy. Warm. Not covered in come so that's a plus, but to see the way he beams up at me... it's so worth it.

"Fuck me, Kylie," he says again, and this time I recognize it as an expletive rather than a command... though, knowing Luca, it's probably both. "I love you so fucking much."

I pop another cucumber cube into my mouth, grinning as I chew. "Back atcha, ace."

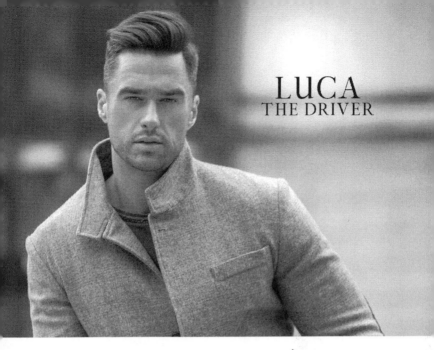

LUCA
THE DRIVER

Ride with the Devil

KYLIE
THE HUMMINGBIRD

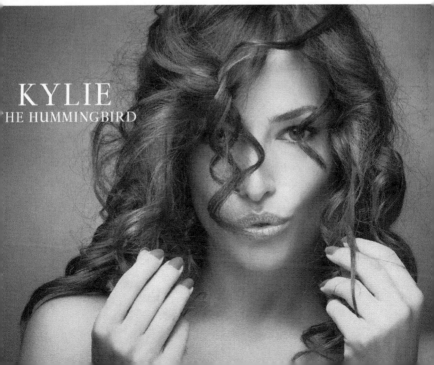

AUTHOR'S NOTE

Thank you for reading *Ride with the Devil*!

Though this does close out the main **Deal with the Devil** series, I love how this book brings readers right back to the first book I wrote for Springfield: *No One Has To Know*. Since this universe began with a woman being taken captive and hidden away in Officer Burns's mountain cabin, I figured it only made sense to end it that way!

Of course, that doesn't mean I'm done with Springfield or these characters forever. I will, however, be shifting to Harmony Heights now, and beginning **The Order of the Owed**, a secret society dark romance series with possessive heroes and the women who learn how to handle them. *Bloody Wedding* is the first full-length book in that world, featuring Adrian Heller, the mysterious man attempting to hire Kylie at the end of this book.

I am also currently working on *Oubliette*, too, telling the story of Haven, the mute heroine who was kept in Winter's cells before Genevieve and Cross were. And if you keep reading/scrolling/clicking, you can get a sneak peek of its cover right now!

xoxo,
Carin

PRE-ORDER NOW

A NEW DARK ROMANCE WITH LOVE, LUST, SECRET SOCIETIES, AND BLOOD...

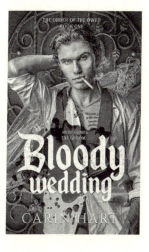

She's always belonged to him. She just didn't know it yet...

LONI

Everyone in Harmony Heights knows about the Order of the Owed. A not-so-secret society, the men who get inducted are set for life. And the women they choose... there's no escape.

I thought I found one. The second I turned eighteen, I was *gone*. A new name. A new start. No expectations. When the day came that the new inductees plotted their lives, I wouldn't be a part of it.

And I believed that for more than a decade—until I received an invitation to my own wedding.

I thought it was a joke. No way was I going to be forced into marrying one of Owed. It wasn't going to happen—

—and, yet, there I was, dressed in white, about to get married to a man I didn't know.

Whoops. Wrong again.

Because the man who walked in on the ceremony, calmly shooting my 'fiancé' before taking his place?

I know *him*.

Adrian Heller. My biggest tormentor... and my biggest secret.

ADRIAN

For too long, I had to hide how I felt about Loni Dougherty. Considering my obsession with her was the biggest open secret in all of Harmony Heights, I didn't do that great of a job.

Everyone knew—except *her*.

She thought I was her high school bully. And maybe I was, but I also made her untouchable. No one could have her, and I wouldn't let anyone hurt her more than I had to.

But once I became one of the Owed, I could make her mine. I held onto that, too, until she disappeared and my new loyalties meant I couldn't chase her out of town.

That doesn't mean I gave up on her, though. And when she gets dragged back to Harmony Heights to be given away to another Owed, I make sure the whole order knows that I claimed her first.

She looks so pretty with blood on her wedding dress and my name on her lips, even if her eyes are filled with hate as she vows to be my bride.

But I don't care about that. Loni is mine, and I'll end anyone who tries to take her away from me again.

* *Bloody Wedding* is a dual-POV dark romance that begins the new **The Order of the Owed** series. With the same possessive dark heroes you've met in the **Deal with the Devil** series, and a secret society twist, it gives new meaning to the phrase: *'til death do us part.*

COMING SOON

WHAT HAPPENED TO HAVEN SMITH?

KEEP IN TOUCH

Stay tuned for what's coming up next! Follow me at any of these places—or sign up for my newsletter—for news, promotions, upcoming releases, and more:

CarinHart.com
Carin's Newsletter
Carin's Signed Book Store

facebook.com/carinhartbooks
amazon.com/author/carinhart
instagram.com/carinhartbooks

ALSO BY CARIN HART

Deal with the Devil series

No One Has To Know *standalone

Silhouette *standalone

He Sees You *standalone

The Devil's Bargain

The Devil's Bride *newsletter exclusive

The Devil's Playground

Dragonfly

Dance with the Devil

Ride with the Devil

Reed Twins

Close to Midnight

Really Should Stay

The Order of the Owed

Oubliette

Bloody Wedding

Inconvenient Marriage

Husband Who

Standalone

My Wife

And the Beast

Made in the USA
Middletown, DE
17 March 2025

72709487R00199